The White Hare

MICHAEL FISHWICK is a publisher and novelist. He has written two other acclaimed novels, *Smashing People* and *Sacrifices*.

The White Hare

Michael Fishwick

ZEPHYR

First published in the UK in 2017 by Zephyr,
an imprint of Head of Zeus, Ltd.

9 7 5 3 1 2 4 6 8

A catalogue record for this book is available from
the British Library.

ISBN (HB): 9781786690517
ISBN (E): 9781786690500

Typeset by Adrian McLaughlin

Printed and bound in Leck, Germany, by CPI Books GmbH

Head of Zeus Ltd
First Floor East
5–8 Hardwick Street
London ECIR 4RG

WWW.HEADOFZEUS.COM

*For my parents, whose lives together
were great adventures*

I

THE CAN – big, dirty, white – was almost too heavy for him. The police never found out where he got it. He couldn't remember anyway. One thing he did remember later was his social worker telling him that fire was his way of expressing his anger about the death of his mum. He said the fire *was* his anger. She'd looked a bit surprised.

The floodlights were off. The kids played there all day and would have played all night, but the rec closed at seven. He kicked his way in where the wire netting was loose, hauling the can after him. He got past the swings and climbed the walkway, spilling petrol, shaking it round the red cabin. The can was easier to handle as it got lighter. The smell stuck in his throat and made him want to throw up. He liked it all the same.

He jumped down and rolled like parachutists do when they land. Then he lit the rag and threw it. Flames rippled along the walkway with a soft moan, and the heat began to push him back towards the fence.

He watched, loving the flames, their wildness and their strength. Then he realized what was happening.

He couldn't get out. The fire was too fierce and he couldn't find the hole in the fence . . .

2

'SHE'S STILL there.'

Robbie was clambering up the hill, his trainers sliding in the mud. It had been raining on and off all day, but it was clear now and there was a full moon. He could hear Mags's voice whispering excitedly.

He scrambled some more, tugging at saplings and bits of bramble, leaves and twigs whipping his face. He could hardly see where he was going or where he was or what was underneath his feet.

Suddenly he was lying beside her on the grass overlooking a field, and he felt her hand on his back pressing him down, so his face, which was probably the only clean bit of him left, got mud all over it.

Mags had been up to the field twice already that night before she'd come and got him. He knew this was a serious thing for her, but he had no idea why.

That was the thing about Mags. She never explained

anything much. Well, at all would be more accurate. When they first met he hated that about her, but he'd hated everyone then, and, to be honest, he still did. Not Mags, though. That had changed.

When he was allowed to raise his face clear of the mud and scrape it from his eyes, Robbie saw, about twenty metres away, something that at first looked to him like a star fallen to earth, dazzling but hard to define.

His eyes focused

'What's that?' he asked. 'I've never seen anything like it.'

'A hare. She's a hare,' said Mags. She was older than him by a few years and treated him like her little brother.

'How do you know it's a she?' he asked, and Mags replied, 'It's her, it's always her.'

Where Robbie grew up they didn't get much wildlife, apart from scrawny urban foxes and fat pigeons, but he could tell a beautiful animal when he saw one. It was odd, he felt he could see this one as if she was closer than she should be, as if she had been magnified.

He screwed his eyes shut and then opened them again. Yes, she was still there.

'I've been waiting a long time for her,' said Mags. 'And now she's come.'

The hare was sitting up on her big back legs with her forelegs out in front, staring dead ahead, but he knew she was aware of everything around her, everything moving and everything still, and probably lots of things he couldn't see or hear, and, this was the strangest bit, maybe even things that could never be seen or heard by ordinary people like him. Every now and then he felt that way about Mags too.

The hare turned her head, and she seemed even closer than before. Her big dark eyes were set high below her sloping forehead and she seemed to be looking straight at him, straight into him. Her ears were long and tapered like a bird's wings, her body hunched like a question mark. She was so bright and so near, and there seemed to be a light about her, whether it was the moon or not he didn't know, but there was light everywhere, the field was flooded with it.

He was suddenly frightened, but the fear wasn't just his. He was sharing it with Mags, and he was sharing it with this beautiful animal so bright and so close and terrified, as if the world was after her, after all three of them. It was the fear of being hunted. That's what it was.

Then she was gone.

Waves of moonlight ebbed away behind her, and he was left with a shadow of sadness.

He shivered.

3

ROBBIE FELT Mags's hand on his back again, urging him to get up, but this time they walked along the edge of the field, following it round until they got to the trees on the other side, and then they went down the path between them.

He asked, 'Why didn't we come up this way? It's a lot easier.'

Mags laughed.

The moonlight spilled over everything, though more faintly, making the woodland look as if at any moment it might dissolve into a mist. A moon mist. Owls were hunting not far away; he could hear their mournful cries piercing the silvery air.

Mags was fishing about in the pocket of her jacket, then she was unlocking a door and turning on a torch and they were in some kind of hut.

Robbie felt a little shaky. In the torchlight

Mags frowned slightly. She was looking for something.

'Where'd she go?' he asked, and of all the things he could have asked this felt right, because Mags stopped hunting through the boxes and half-empty tool kits and shone the torch in his face.

'We don't know,' she said. 'We never know. However hard we try.'

There was the scraping of a match and a little *whoosh* in the corner. She had lit a camping stove and was heating a kettle, and Robbie asked her if she had anything stronger, in case there was something hidden under a floorboard, but she shook her head.

So they both had instant black coffee in cups that looked as if they could have done with a wash.

'How's your dad? Did he get that job?' Robbie asked after a while.

Mags shook her head again.

'And your mum?'

'Well, you know, she's still cleaning, so that looks all right. Her new man likes her to work. He's okay, though.'

'Your dad doesn't try very hard, does he? He'd be a lot better off with someone around the home, wouldn't he? Just to get him out of it, maybe?' This time Mags nodded. But it wasn't going to be her tidying up after her dad and sorting out his mess. There wasn't much in it, but she'd chosen to live with her mum, and that was that. At least she had one.

Anyway, Mags was crazy about animals and she was especially crazy about hares. He'd learned that much about her. She used to keep them as pets when she was younger, before her parents split up and they moved out of the house, and her mother ended up living on the other side of the village with someone who did the same kind of odd-jobbing for the farms that Mags's dad did and who didn't even look very different. Mags said she didn't know why her mum bothered, and Robbie said perhaps she just wanted a change. Mags nodded slowly and blew out her cheeks and said maybe that was it. Now all her dad did was sit in front of his TV, drink too much and stick out his lower lip.

'So what was that you said? "We don't know where the hare goes." Who's we?'

Mags tensed and something came down sharply between them. 'People,' she said quietly to herself.

She was small, scrappy and lean. She was wearing a green cotton jacket with epaulettes and lots of pockets, skinny jeans tucked into Doc Marten boots and her favourite black belt with a silver skull buckle. Silver studs shone in her ears. A grey flat cap hid her hair, which was like honey, or the corn at the end of the summer, and which she wore tied up. Wisps always straggled down her neck, and despite being younger Robbie felt protective of her. He would never have dared show it though. She was much too proud for that sort of thing. She had a way of looking sideways with her large pale blue eyes, which seemed to change colour in different lights, then looking away again very quickly, a flicker of a look, checking you out, especially if she'd just met you. Which for Robbie was down by the bridge soon after they came to live in Somerset, when his dad and Sheila were busy doing up the new house.

The bridge – their bridge – wasn't far from the house. It was a cattle bridge, really, the earth on either side pitted by hooves, and it crossed the river that ran through the village. It was a perfect place for a quiet smoke, leaning against the railings with the water sidling underneath and the trees crowding in from the banks.

She was sitting on one of the lower railings of the bridge the way she always liked to, with her arms folded on the top one and her legs dangling from the lower. Robbie wondered whether to say hi or just walk past. She glanced at him, then went back to contemplating the water and he thought she was going to ignore him. He'd just crossed over when he heard her voice.

'Going to say hello?'

He turned.

'Have we met?'

'No, we haven't. But I know who you are. And you can say hello to strangers. It's polite.'

She raised her eyebrows and he found himself smiling.

'Hi,' he said. 'I'm new here.'

She could have told him they were living in the house she'd lived in all her life. Her family had been tenants there, and it was a wreck. Peeling wallpaper, rotting window frames, an old caravan in the garden, corrugated iron everywhere. Now it was being transformed. All cosy with new carpets and stripped floorboards, spotlights in the ceiling and a steel-coloured oven and a steel-coloured fridge that made ice. The only old thing, apart from the yellow stones of the house itself, which glowed in the evening sun, was the grandfather clock on the landing that had been in his dad's family for years.

She could have told him how much she had loved that house, just the way it had been. She could have made him feel guilty. But she didn't. She watched him for a moment, in her green jacket and battered jeans and brown boots, which were like a kind of camouflage, as if she was blending into the dark leaves and the bank and the water below. Or maybe it was as though she was an element of everything around her, a pale blonde ghost caught between where she was and where she'd come from. She untied her hair – he could see she bit her nails – and tied it up again, balancing on the rail, eyes flickering, chewing him over.

As they talked he'd thought, she's a bit weird, this one.

But then he wasn't exactly normal, was he?

Robbie was clever, but he was trouble too, at least that's what the judge had said. He knew the things he'd done were wrong and he didn't want to go back there, but sometimes he wanted to explode and burn like he used to. Sometimes he didn't know how he was holding it all in, home being the way it was. Nothing much had changed, he'd just swapped tarmac and high-rise for fields, and they didn't make him any calmer. In fact, they terrified him.

So he was running away from home and running away from fields. Sometimes he thought he should run away properly, run away and not stop, and he would have done if it wasn't for Mags. Being around her made him feel better, brought out his clever side, perhaps. He liked to be reminded that there was something good about himself.

He'd once asked Mags why she didn't keep hares as pets any more, and she'd said she thought it was cruel.

'But they used to do it,' he said. 'There was this poet who wrote about having one that played on his carpet and was called Puss. We read it in school once.'

Without looking at him she said, 'You're actually quite smart, aren't you?' And he liked that because he knew she meant it. Then she said that Puss was one of the names that hares had, and she told him some others too, chanting them slowly, like a spell.

'The hare-ling, the frisky one,
Old Turpin, the fast traveller.'

They were standing near her house, waiting for her mum to get back. It was warm, and Mags's eyes burned a kind of purple-blue. She was looking at a wood about a hundred metres away over a field that hadn't had crops that year, just grazing.

'The lurker in ditches, the filthy beast,
The one who doesn't go straight home, the traitor,
The friendless one, the cat of the wood.'

Her words and the pictures they made flew round Robbie's head, and the stillness in the air felt like a pulse beating.

'The stag with the leathery horns,
The animal that dwells in the corn,
The animal that all men scorn,
The animal that no one dare name.'

The words flew on, round and round, and the pictures, until he thought they would go on forever. They tumbled through his thoughts. *Hare-ling. Lurker. Cat of the wood. Leathery horns.*

  'That's an older poem than the one I know,' Robbie said when she'd finished.

'Yes, I think it is,' she'd replied.

He thought of asking her to say it again, but he also thought, maybe that's enough, maybe I am filled up enough with words and pictures. And, anyway, he sort of knew she wouldn't.

She said, 'They do box, you know.' She smiled, because she could see he didn't understand what she was talking about. 'Boxing. Hares are famous for it. Lots of people say it's untrue, but it's not. I've seen it. They sit around in a circle, and now and then a pair of them leap at each other and stand up on their hind legs and box each other with their forepaws. They do it in the spring. I'll show you.'

She looked at him thoughtfully.

'They know they're graceful, you can see it in their eyes.'

The light in the shed was dimming as the torch's batteries began to fade. Mags had lots of haunts like this one, in old barns and even in holes in trees, where she kept things or laid low, when things used to get bad at home. She was a girl with a lot of hiding places.

She gave the cups a wipe with her finger, then started pulling at a big crate in the corner.

'Come on,' she said. 'Help me.' At first he didn't understand what she was doing, then he saw the crate had handles at either end, so he grabbed one and hauled on it. As they carried it towards the door he saw it wasn't a crate but a cage. Inside was something like a tablecloth, neatly folded and quite plain, though he couldn't make out the colour in the torchlight or in the moonlight when they got outside. It was darker than when they'd arrived, the moon was closer to the horizon and the trees were black against it. They carried the cage along the path away from the village.

'It's for her,' she said. 'If I find her. To keep her safe.' Then she murmured to herself, 'If I can.'

When they got to where they were going, she made him swear not to tell anyone. He didn't tell her that he was the last person she should be sharing secrets with, but he did say where are we, and how are we going to get back, and I'm going to be in loads of trouble, and are you going to tell me what this is about? He was feeling really tired, but most of all ignorant, and he didn't like either.

Then he felt her take his hand in the darkness, and he pulled away, but she held on and said, 'Don't worry,' and for once in his life he didn't. That's the way it was with Mags. She put out his fires.

4

IT WAS all right for Mags to say don't worry – it was always fine when he was with her – but he had to go home.

It was so late when he got back that he was surprised to find his dad was still up, sitting there with a face like a rainy day. He yelled at Robbie about how worried he and Sheila had been.

'Sheila's so worried she's in bed asleep, Dad, I can hear her snoring,' Robbie replied.

His dad hated that. Robbie meant him to.

Next morning Robbie came downstairs singing softly to himself. Like Mum. She always used to sing, no matter what she was doing. He pulled on his jacket to go out. The kitchen door opened behind him.

'I don't think you'll be needing that, Robbie.'

Robbie turned to see his dad blocking the way. He stopped singing.

'I'm going out, Dad,' he said. ''Scuse me.' He went to push past and they scuffled, because his dad was trying not to unfold his arms and lose his dignity. His dad let his body sway to one side to narrow the gap, and, too late, realized that wasn't going to be enough and had to make a lunge at the last moment. But then Sheila sailed out of the kitchen where she had been listening and Robbie was outnumbered.

He knew what was coming next. A round-the-kitchen-table-what-shall-we-do-about-Robbie session. He pushed back a lock of black curling hair and narrowed his eyes, running his tongue over his lips. For all his misgivings, there was a determined look about him, a wiliness, almost a slyness. He had dark eyes, good cheekbones and a chin that didn't look as if he would take no for an answer. He stuck his hands deep into the pockets of his jeans, planted his feet in their mud-caked blue-and-white Air Max trainers well apart, and waited.

'We just don't know what we're going to do with you.'

'Frankly, I'm nearing the end of my tether.'

'Personally, I've reached the end of mine.'

'We thought that bringing you here would help you, but it doesn't seem to be having much effect. We only came for your sake.'

That's a lie, Dad, thought Robbie. You grew up here and Sheila wanted to start over.

'Maybe the new school is the problem.'

Of course it is, he thought. It's full of kids I don't know and I don't understand a word they're saying. I don't understand their accents and I don't get their world.

'I thought the countryside would have a calming effect.'

'Half the time we just don't know where you are.'

'Out till all hours,' said Sheila. 'And we know where that kind of behaviour leads.'

'We just can't go on like this.'

'We get nothing back from you, despite everything we've done.'

'You don't seem to care about other people, especially your family.'

'Arrogance, that's all it is. Pure and simple.'

'And immaturity.'

'And immaturity.'

He had been convicted of arson and sentenced to a Youth Rehabilitation Order, he deserved better than this.

Sheila was the choker in everything. She filled the house like a cloud, pressing against the walls, clogging the stairs, rubbing against the ceilings, curling down pipes, seeping under the beds and coiling round his throat. She made him feel breathless. Lots of things can make you feel breathless: excitement, terror, unhappy situations. Sheila was an unhappy situation. Sheila was an unhappy situation that wanted him out, out of this house, out of her life.

She got up and put her hand on her hip and arched slightly, grimacing with pain. His dad gave her a worried look, then his face softened and he tilted his head as if to ask if she was all right. To Robbie's disgust she stood behind his dad and placed both hands on his shoulders to take the weight off her feet, then stroked his head and hobbled over to the kettle.

'This sort of thing's no good for my back,' she said.

'Hypochondriac,' said Robbie, going too far and conjuring a firestorm of angry retribution. The result was predictable, in fact, inevitable. It had been coming all along. Not allowed to leave the house without telling them where he was going. Curfew at six etc.

'The garden?' he asked wearily.

'What about it?' said his dad.

'Can I go into the garden?' He couldn't stand the house, he couldn't stand the fields; he had to go somewhere.

His dad said yes before Sheila could intervene. Robbie leaped from his chair and ran to the back door.

5

DESPITE HIMSELF, Robbie liked the garden and how tumbled it was because Sheila and his dad hadn't got round to doing anything to it yet. It was large enough to lose himself in, and there were apple trees and plum trees, their fruit good enough to eat, not that anyone picked it. The previous autumn the apples and plums had lain in the long grass and rotted, tunnelled and feasted upon by thousands of wasps.

Soon he was among the trees clustered at the end of the garden and he went through them to the wall at the end, where he could hardly see the house. There was a field beyond the boundary wall, and an old tree stump, where he could sit down and have a cigarette. The smell would hang about his clothes, and his dad and Sheila would notice but pretend not to.

He texted Mags to see if she was around, though she left her phone off a lot of the time and he wasn't surprised he didn't get a reply. So he texted some friends back home and a girl in his class called Alice, the only one he talked to, but everyone seemed to be asleep.

There was a movement in the next-door garden, and he could just see a slight shape, Mrs Allardyce, doing something to her compost heap. Mr Allardyce had a telescope and studied the stars at night, and sometimes he let Robbie look. A week ago they had studied the rings of Saturn for an hour, clear and beautiful, very small and very far away.

Mags didn't seem to be sure about the Allardyces, though they were friendly to Robbie. She told him to be careful when he was talking to them. 'They're not quite the way they seem,' she had said.

So he was sitting watching Mrs Allardyce and then looking way up the field over the wall where the grass was cropped so close that it felt soft, almost comforting to walk on, but he could feel the anger welling up. He never used to listen to his social worker, though one thing he remembered was that she had said it would all get better in time. How long is time? he thought to himself. Long, maybe forever. As long as it takes to get to Saturn?

She'd also told him that his anger was his way of trying to deal with all the sadness and loss.

He thought, where does that get you?

Of course he was sad his mum died, and she took

so long to do it, until he thought maybe he would die first. And then she did, and he hadn't been there, and the feeling that because of that he had failed her tore him apart. He thought maybe he did die for a bit then. Perhaps it was only anger that had kept him alive. He supposed he must have wanted to be alive, because the anger never left him. It just eventually went somewhere else, like when they have a fire at a coal mine and they put it out, but it goes on burning along the seam.

His phone went. Mags.

'Where are you?'

'I'm grounded,' he said.

Mags said she wasn't surprised and she was sorry, which was fair enough, because it was kind of her fault. And Robbie said don't worry about it, and she asked what he was going to do, and he said he thought he'd better just stay where he was for a while.

'There's something I want you to see,' she said.

'Don't think I can, Mags.'

'It's important. Come on, we don't have much time.'

'What is it? It'd better be good.'

'I don't know why they're doing this to you, anyway.'

'It's Sheila. She's a witch.'

'Don't say that.'

'Well, she is.'

'You don't know what you're saying. I mean, you really don't. Trust me. I'll be there in five.'

So they ended up half-walking, half-running down the road to a turning where the road rose steeply under high hedgerows to the top where there was a field and then another field, ploughed, the earth covered with the prickle of a new crop. Robbie felt a rush of exhilaration. He could see the buds chasing along the branches of the trees. He could feel life coming back. The fields and the hills glimmered green, and there was birdsong, and Robbie thought, this is all so new, and still so new to me.

Mags leaned against the gate and they watched. The field sloped down to some trees on the far side, and on this side of them was a ring of hares, about ten of them. Some were sitting on their haunches, some were lying down, not paying attention, but two or three were inside the circle, thumping the ground with their back feet. He could hear it faintly but clearly. It must have been something to do with the acoustics; the field had a wide, shallow dip like a saucer, which seemed to amplify every sound. Every now and then two of the hares reared on their hind legs and punched at each other. Soon more arrived, making new circles full of lunging, jumping, kicking hares, and they started running after each other, round and round.

'Do they always do this?' Robbie asked Mags, and she shook her head.

'Loners from the day they're born,' she said. 'And they're mostly nocturnal. They make these circles, but they're not common, and I've never seen anything like this many.'

'So why's it happening?'

'It must be because she's here.'

'Where? I can't see her,' he said, but Mags didn't answer.

'Are they waiting for her?' he went on, and Mags said she didn't know, she didn't know everything. Then she said, 'They're running against the sun.'

'Meaning being?'

'Widdershins. Anti-clockwise. Trouble's coming. It always does.'

There was something in the tone of her voice, as if maybe she wanted it.

What was going through that head of hers? he wondered.

He needed to get back.

'Don't tell anyone you saw this,' Mags said to him, holding him by his jacket as he tried to run. 'It's important. You don't know how important. Swear.'

Robbie thought, that's the second time she's asked me to do that.

When he got back there was a text from her that said, 'Meet at beacon when free.'

He went to see his dad.

'I can't do this any more,' he said. The feeling

had been building up inside him for weeks, and that morning's tussle with Dad and Sheila had made it almost unbearable.

They were standing together outside the back of the house, where the thatching hung over the kitchen door. Side by side, they looked more alike than Robbie would have wanted to believe, though where Robbie let his hair run long, his father's was more conventional, if a little prone to untidiness, and its darkness was turning white at the temples.

It was quiet there, away from the road. They could see all the way down the garden, down the wide path through the orchard to the wall and the field beyond. His dad was looking along it and hadn't seemed to hear him, so Robbie said it again. His dad turned.

Robbie had never seen this expression on his dad's face before. He looked scared, as if he'd heard bad news, or remembered something he didn't want to.

And he said, 'I'm afraid I can't help you.'

Robbie walked down the path to the end of the garden, thinking, he'll call me back. Maybe I'll go. Why am I being like this? Maybe I won't go. This time I won't. Why should I?

His dad didn't call.

Come on, Dad. I need you now.

Beyond the wall, there was a flicker of white chasing across the field.

Robbie blinked. It was still there.

He blinked again. It had gone.

Was it chasing, or was it being chased?

Perhaps that was what his dad had seen. He tried to think what his expression had reminded him of. Then he got it.

It was as if he'd seen a ghost.

There'd been a time when they used to do lots of great things together, he and his dad. They used to go swimming in a huge open-air lido, one where the queue seemed endless on days when it was hot. When you got in, the water seemed to go on for miles and was crowded but cold and felt amazing, and just what you needed. Then you warmed up and it was even better.

They used to go to films too, at the local cinema, doing the whole Coke and popcorn thing, sitting in the darkness, waiting for happiness to begin.

The other thing his dad loved was going fishing, something he'd learned in the rivers and pools where they lived now. He was a natural, whatever the water, whatever the method. Flies or floats or leger, he was expert at them all. There are places in London you can fish – they're hard to find but they're there – and they tend to be packed as full as the lidos. But usually they would drive out to somewhere, and if it was a river, his dad got out all these beautiful flies with names like Tupp's Indefensible or Parachute Adams.

He kept them in little plastic boxes, and then he'd head off along the bank, crouching down and feeding the line out over the water. It was like what Mags said about hares: he was graceful, beautiful to watch, and he could land a fly just where he wanted it, even when they were surrounded by trees and bushes.

His dad had just been beginning to teach him how to tie on flies and floats and weights and hooks, and how to use ground-bait, and where fish like to lie, and how to go for the fat bottom-feeders like carp, and where to find the big roach rather than those scrappy little ones that take your bait if you're not careful, when his mum got ill. And Sheila came along, and they'd ended up down here, and blah, blah. Sheila wanted the country life with her daughters, Jess and Lucy, and they wanted to get Robbie away from a place that was obviously not doing him much good. Also, Sheila had been a teacher at Robbie's school, and when he thought about it he was never quite sure when her relationship with his father had begun. Perhaps Sheila was more than happy to leave such mysteries behind.

Now, he and his dad never went fishing.

6

'WHAT'S THAT bubbling sound?' He could just hear it in spite of the wind.

'Larks. Two of them. Look, one's falling.' Mags was happy. 'Up here you can see everything.'

'Why's it called the beacon, then?'

'In the old days, when England was being invaded, they'd light fires on all the high hills. This is one of them.'

Fires burning everywhere. Robbie liked the sound of that.

'Couldn't've happened very often.'

'When the Spanish came.'

'You learned something in school, then, Mags.'

'1588. The Armada. Only date I can remember.'

'1066?'

'Isn't that Kronenbourg?'

They were sitting on grass that was short and springy

because of the sheep, backs to a big grey rock. The wind was in Mags's hair, and she kept trying to stop it flying out in front of her, pushing it behind her ears and constantly readjusting the light blue band that was keeping most of it bunched together. The rock was cold against Robbie's shoulders. He scrunched up his long eyelashes and his thick eyebrows against the sunshine.

The old beacon was on a hill that jutted out from a long line, an escarpment overlooking the Levels towards the Tor. There were woods on top of the scarp, punctuated by white flowering blackthorn, that looked as if they had been striding towards the edge and had just stopped in time. Some had spilled over and littered the drop. There were none on the beacon hill itself, though its slopes were spangled with daisies and dandelions. In front of them the land flattened until it reached another line of hills, miles and miles away, small and grey and misty. From the fields below came the anxious yelling of lambs, and not far away a kestrel hovered. Up here on the beacon the wind was chilly and unpredictable. Mags didn't seem to notice it as much as Robbie, not because of her clothes, he found himself thinking, but just because she was Mags. She was hard stone.

There were lots of hollows all around them. The hill was pitted like an enormous green golf ball. When Robbie asked about them, Mags said they were old mine-workings.

'People used to dig stuff out of the ground. They used to live up here too.'

'What, recently?'

'Muppet. Thousands of years ago.'

'Stone Age people?'

She nodded. 'I'll show you one of their houses.'

She started telling him about the things they could see below them. Robbie didn't particularly mind getting a geography lesson from Mags. As the junior partner in the relationship he got a lot of this.

'See that big hill with the flat top and hardly any trees and all those earthworks on it? That's Cadbury Castle, King Arthur's Camelot, and inside the hill King Arthur and his knights are sleeping. Every Midsummer Eve and Christmas Eve they ride out through the golden gates along the old track to the well in the woods where their horses can drink. People have heard them riding by. I've heard them myself. The Atwells own all the fields between there and us. And the road that runs beyond it is Dancing Lane.'

'Why's it called that?'

''Cos that's where they hung people, and when you get hung and you die your legs start to go everywhere and it looks like you're dancing.'

'Nice.'

'Then those fields down there are owned by the

Grants, well, used to be, he's the only one left now, lives on his own and he's completely mental. That's what living on your own does to you.'

Robbie guessed she might have her dad in mind.

'Where's our village from here?'

'Way over there towards Cary.'

He thought for a bit.

'Mags?'

'Uh huh?'

'That poem. The one about the hares. What did all those names mean?'

A doting look came into her eyes. For once he'd asked the right question.

'You mean?'

And she began to chant, in a voice that half-spoke, half-sang:

> 'The hare-ling, the frisky one,
> Old Turpin, the fast traveller,
> The way-beater, the white-spotted one.'

Once again, the words seemed to work on Robbie like a spell. A feeling of peace spread through his body and he could feel the tension go. The world felt calmer. He could even have sworn the wind was gentler. Less bullying, less harsh.

'I don't know all of it,' said Mags, 'and there's loads more:

> *'The wild animal, the jumper,*
> *The short animal, the lurker,*
> *The swift-as-wind, the skulker,*
> *The dew-beater, the dew-hopper.'*

'Dew-hopper is 'cos they feed in the early morning and late evening, and you can see their tracks in the dew. Skulking is what they do when they're frightened, their ears go flat against their heads and they crouch low to the ground.'

'What about Turpin? Is that like the highwayman?'

'Turpin is what they used to call a highwayman, any kind of scallywag. The white-spotted one is about the spots some hares have on their faces, they're supposed to have the same number of babies.'

'Can we have some more?'

She half-sang again:

> *'The lurker in ditches, the filthy beast,*
> *The one who doesn't go straight home, the traitor,*
> *The friendless one, the cat of the wood,*
> *The starer with wide eyes.'*

'Hares never go straight home 'cos they're always doubling back on themselves as they run. And they're supposed to sleep with their eyes open, though how anyone would know that, I don't know. You can't sneak up on a sleeping hare, they'd smell you a mile off.'

'And they do stare and they do have wide eyes. 'Least, the one we saw had. And what was that bit about a stag I remember?'

'The stag with the leathery horns. I don't know about that one – maybe once people thought they did have horns. Maybe they thought they were like little deer. Or their ears were like horns. Anyway, it's weird, 'cos at the end it's the animal that no one dare name, and you get all these names before that, so it's like some kind of joke.'

'Or a riddle, or a mystery.'

'They're mysterious, all right. Strangest animals I know.'

'And the white hare?'

She squinted at him quickly like she did when she was uncertain. Then she huddled herself together and put her head back against the rock and said nothing. Robbie was beginning to think she'd clammed up for good when she suddenly relaxed, as if she'd been holding her breath all along, and said, 'You really want to know?'

''Course.'

'Okay. The white hare . . .' She stopped and started pulling up little clumps of grass and throwing them, so they got caught by the wind and flew from sight. Robbie could see there was something wrong.

'Mags . . .'

'It's okay, it's okay,' she said quickly. Then, as if she was trying to keep something down, as if she was quoting something, she continued, 'When a woman dies abandoned by her lover she can return in the shape of a white hare.'

'When a woman dies abandoned by her lover,' he repeated.

'Yes. That's what they say. When a woman dies of a broken heart, or when in the old days she's been jilted, you know, left at the altar or her expectations denied, and she goes to rack and ruin and solitary death in a dirty old room mourned by nobody. Or if . . .' Her voice drifted to a halt, and she looked away down the hill at something.

'Or if?' he asked.

Her face screwed up into a ball for a moment, and she swallowed. 'Or if she takes her own life.' He could hardly hear her.

'You've got to love someone a lot to do that.'

'Well, I know one that did.'

'Who?'

'No one you'd have heard of.'

He thought about this, and thought about the legend. 'So she can return as a white hare? I mean, they say?'

'Not everyone can see her, but the lover always can.'

'Okay.'

He must have sounded doubtful, because she scowled at him.

'Believe what you want,' she snapped. 'It's very old, I know that. I've told you now.'

'No, I believe you, I believe you.'

He found himself remembering his dad outside the back door, that look on his face, something white far away on the hill. As if he'd seen a ghost.

And then he thought, wait.

'But I could see her.'

'Yeah. Yeah, you could. That's interesting. I mean, you haven't dumped anyone recently, have you?'

They both started to laugh, a little bit hysterically.

And you could see her too, Mags, so what's that all about?

Robbie got up and shook himself and ran down into the first hollow and up the other side.

'Come on, Mags, let's go.'

There was sunlight on the fields between the racing shadows of the clouds. To Robbie it felt as if they were floating in the air up there, so far away from what was going on below. Yet looking out over the world everything seemed more in focus, closer.

Down in Dancing Lane he could see an old Land Rover beetling along to a gate. Someone, a young man with curly hair, got out to open it, then they drove to the low shoulder of a hill and disappeared round the other side.

'Who lives over there?'

'It's not that way, it's this.' Now it was Mags who seemed eager to go, tugging at his sleeve.

'Who lives over there, at the end of that lane?'

She didn't answer. Maybe she didn't hear. Maybe she didn't want to hear.

But as they set off she turned and squinted quickly back to where he had been pointing, muttering something and giving a small shake of her head.

She'd been looking there when she'd been talking about the person she knew who'd killed herself.

She leaped over the lip of a hollow and disappeared, and Robbie went with her. There was no wind. Robbie crouched next to Mags for a while, until he noticed the mouth of a passage opposite set deep in the turf. At the end it appeared to dive into a kind of small chamber that was lined with stones, its floor bare earth covered with sheep droppings.

'What's that?'

'I told you. It's where they used to live. The old people.'

'It can't be.'

She jerked her head forwards, stubborn as ever.

'If you say so, Mags.'

After a while they picked themselves up and went inside.

Mags seemed at home. Another one of her hiding places Robbie thought. It wasn't much to look at, stones had fallen out of the walls and no one had bothered to put them back. Mags was gently touching the ones that were left, as if she was making sure they were where they should be. There was a stone slab on the ground by the wall in one corner, worn smooth. Mags threw herself down on it and lay staring up. Robbie sat on the floor, taking care to keep well clear of the droppings.

'This is a good place,' she said. 'We used to come here, Fran and me.'

'Who's Fran?'

'The one I told you about.'

'The one who—?'

'Yes. I haven't been back here since then.'

'What's it called?'

'It's not called anything. Not now.'

The place that no one dare name.

The sun's warmth was stealing in as the day wore on. Outside sheep were bleating.

Yes, feels like a good place.

'Mags?'

'Mm?'

'Do you ever think about how you want your life to turn out?'

'Yup. I want to live in a castle and fill all the rooms with my favourite animals.'

'Seriously?'

'Yeah. What's *your* dream, though?'

'Just want my mum back.' He thought this every day, but this was the first time he'd said it out loud to anyone.

Mags went over and put her arms around him.

'I can't imagine what it's like,' she said.

He didn't cry so much any more, nothing like he used to. He just seized up in his head when he thought about it, which was almost preferable.

Sometimes, though, he thought he caught sight of his mum in the street in town among the crowds, or standing at the end of a lane, and his heart leaped.

The thing about tears, he noticed, was how they would start from your eyes wet and cold, then, after a while, as more and more ran down your face, they would dry out, but you could still feel their tracks as if there were warm ghost fingers cradling your cheeks.

He'd been dreaming a lot recently. He never used to dream that much before, hardly at all, in fact. And in these dreams he saw his mum, and it wasn't quite true about him not crying so much, because when he woke up the pillow was wet.

Mags's face was soft against his.

There was a sound outside.

'We'd better go, Mags,' he said. 'There's someone coming.'

'How do you know?'

'I can hear a voice.'

'Can you? You sure?'

He listened.

'Yeah. Someone singing.' He thought for a moment, listening hard. 'It's strange. It's like the way you were singing, just now.'

'There's no one there. Isn't it beautiful here, though, Robbie?'

'Top. Let's go.'

She sighed. 'There's no one there. Believe me. No one.' She sounded sad. Then she got up and smiled at him as if she knew something he didn't. 'Okay.'

He was surprised. She didn't usually do things he asked.

Outside the sheep crowded round, hemming them in.

Mags smiled at him again. 'Nobody but us and the sheep.'

She took his hand and they walked to the road.

'I'd better go back,' he said, and dread surged inside him. Back to his happy home.

He turned to look behind one last time, at the world sunning itself for miles and miles, buffeted by the fitful wind.

There was someone there after all. A girl. For a moment he couldn't tell how far away she was. She seemed closer than she should be. The sun was getting in his eyes, blinding him.

'Hey, I was right, look.'

But Mags was too far ahead.

And when he looked again, all he could see was the sheep grazing.

7

THE FIRST time Robbie knew there was something wrong with his mum they had been in the super-market. He had commandeered the trolley, jumping on the back, gunning down the aisles while Mum tried to choose between pepperoni and *quattro formaggio*. When he'd reached the end of the frozen foods aisle, he'd turned the trolley, seen no sign of her and rode it back again, wondering where she had gone.

He went on standing there, looking at everybody and waiting for his mum to turn up, until he thought he'd better go and look for her. Suddenly everything was much bigger than before, the trolley and the bright freezers with all the red meat in shiny plastic, and it was cold, and he began to shiver. He panicked. He was just beginning to run when a hand stopped the trolley and someone said, 'I'm afraid your mum's had a fall.'

People were leaning over her, and she was sitting

up being supported on either side. She was white, white like everything in a supermarket's white, but white mixed with grey so she looked like a crumpled newspaper on a street, and she looked much, much older. She'd smiled at him as though she'd forgotten how to, and her eyes were watery. She stroked his hand, and he saw that hers was trembling. He didn't know whether to hug her or not, he'd never seen her like this. Then she put out her hand again, and he did hug her, but she didn't hug him back properly. He was so glad to have found her he went on hugging her just the same, and she patted him on the back, and said, 'Sorry, darling, must have tripped over something.'

Then the ambulance came, and as they helped her away she gave him a little wave, and after that the shop assistants looked after him until his dad came to fetch him. They gave him more sweets than he'd ever seen before, and he ate them until he felt sick.

Things seemed okay for a while, until one day he'd been waiting for his mum in the playground at school – this was his best moment of the day, when she stood chatting at the gate and he'd be playing football or some game that meant he could show off how fast he was and he knew she'd be watching him – but on this day a stranger came towards him and said, 'Come on, Robbie, let's go,' and for a second he thought he was being kidnapped. Then something clicked and he saw it was his mum, only her hair was blonde and she looked so different he hadn't recognized her. He didn't realize it wasn't her own.

Then, after that, he couldn't remember how long, his dad came into his room and sat at the end of his bed. He'd patted Robbie's leg through the duvet in a tentative sort of way and Robbie knew immediately that something was wrong. His dad never, ever did things like that.

'Mum is going into hospital for a few days,' he'd said. Robbie was terrified. He couldn't imagine what a few days without her would be like. He'd become so agitated he frightened his dad, who clutched him by his arms, and whether he was trying to comfort him, or hold him down, neither of them knew.

Hospital. He got to know it inside out. Endless corridors, scrubbed and polished until the floors and walls were wearing thin, stuffed with nearly dead people being pushed on trolleys or not-really-alive ones shuffling around in dressing gowns and bandages. He remembered walking and walking, looking for the ward with his mum in it, past the chapel of rest and the garden of quietness with the pond full of giant goldfish, and room after room with strange-looking machines inside.

Then at last he'd find her. Sometimes she'd be too weak to move, sometimes she'd be bright smiles all for him, talking as if he was the one in trouble, doing anything to cheer him up. But she seemed to be melting away as he watched, her lovely face now moon-shaped, anxiety clouding her serious grey eyes.

And when she'd come home she was still in bed, and nurses came to look after her, so his home got to be like the hospital, like another bit of it, and his dad was kind of the receptionist, only the receptionist usually knows what's going on.

Robbie would get out just to get out and stay out, that's where it all started. He had a lot of mates, good and bad, smart and not so smart, but he liked hanging out with all of them.

Usually he would be down at the huge rec on the estate. They had giant walkways there, where the older crew hung out, and there were swings and roundabouts coloured yellow and red for the kids. At the other end the wall was a sludge colour where the council had tried to clean off the graffiti too many times. There was a never-ending game of football, and the kids who played in it were brilliant. There was a tiny one who was a cripple, and he swung around on crutches, better than anyone, untouchable. If any of them had played for England we might have won something, Robbie thought.

You couldn't just play, though, you had to wait till they liked you. He was useless at first, but he worked at it until he could do a few tricks and then he found he could play all he wanted to. He was fast, very fast, and he could run round anyone.

Robbie wasn't really part of it all, he just kidded himself he was to make himself feel better, and they let him. All of them knew about his mum and he knew they felt sorry for him. They were good friends at a bad time that was going to get a lot worse. Most of the big kids stayed at the other end of the rec. The walkways and cabins and stuff where the kids were supposed to be able to go was their territory. Sometimes someone in a peaked cap came along and tried to move them on, sometimes the police did. The meanest of them, Ali, lived in a red cabin on stilts meant for eight-year-olds, and smoked all day, and his crew spread about him, in a vague hierarchy. He always had some little distraction going on. Mostly setting fire to things; bins, normally. Robbie used to join in. Ali would break open a few lighters, pour the insides over a bit of tissue and drop it in a bin, then throw a lighted match in after it, and the whole thing would go off, *pop*.

Robbie loved watching those bins go up. Once they set fire to five in a row.

He got a taste for it.

Then one day he got back home to find his dad standing in the kitchen with a stretched look on his face and he knew what had happened before he opened his mouth. And after that . . . well.

Robbie couldn't bear to go on living in that house. He was obsessed, he wanted the whole world in flames. He went and lit up a line of bikes, they were twisted skeletons after their tanks exploded. The plastic melted and they fell into each other.

Magic, Robbie thought.

He never thought she'd die. He never thought she'd never be there again. He thought she'd get better.

He thought maybe it was his fault. Maybe he shouldn't have been with his friends, maybe he should have been with her in hospital more. He thought maybe this was a punishment for something, but he couldn't work out what. All he knew was that the person who was always going to look after him wasn't there any more. He hadn't really thought about the word 'never' before, but suddenly it was always in his head. Never see her again. Never have her hug him, kiss his cheek, ask him how he was, tell him what to do, make everything all right, cook his favourite food (like macaroni cheese), take him clothes shopping for a treat, scold him into bed when it was late and he was poring over his laptop, help him with his maths homework. That wasn't going to happen. Was never going to happen.

Home wasn't home any more, it was just a collection of objects. Chairs and tables, books, bags, knives and forks in rooms that seemed to echo back at him. So he went on staying away.

Until the night he got caught.

8

THESE DAYS, strangely, one of Robbie's favourite things was the journey to his school. Not being at school, particularly, though the lessons were fine, no better, no worse than at the last one. Just going there and coming back was what he liked. He and everyone else from the village went on the bus, and he could sit at the back and disappear into himself. The others all sat together, but Robbie loved being on his own, enjoying the places in between, when he was neither here nor there, and could watch the fields and hedges go past and sometimes listen to the branches of the trees drumming along the top of the bus.

One good thing about school was that no one knew much about him, though maybe that was a bad thing too, because they didn't want to know, they just left him alone. It had been Mags's school until the previous year when she'd bailed. It was just not for her, she said. He'd asked her, why didn't you stay, you could have been a vet, but she wasn't interested. She knew more than a vet already, animals just loved her; they treated her as if she was one of them. Horses, dogs, cats, cows, pigs, whatever, they all wanted to be her best friend. She held out her hand with its bitten nails and they started sniffing at it and nudging up to her, it almost made Robbie jealous.

There was a girl in his class he liked to talk to, they hung out together. He'd noticed her the first day he turned up, which was not surprising because in a school of what seemed like a million, there were only three black kids and she was one of them, and the sight of her made him homesick for London. Like him she was new, and her name was Alice. She wore her hair in long plaits with lots of coloured beads in them, and she had a solemn look, big eyes full of the sorrows of the world, and she sat with her hands clasped in front of her staring at the teachers as if they could help her learn to save the planet.

Of course she got picked on, so did he, they both did. A bit of shoving, a bit of sniggering behind his back, a lot of name-calling. It wore him down. There was a group of them that did it, there always is, the usual combination of some big insecure creep with small eyes and some kids who followed him around. It got so Robbie started holding a knife again, which he'd stopped because it only gets you into trouble, but he was in trouble, anyway.

'You really need that?' asked Alice when he told her. 'They're not that bad, are they? Just annoying.'

Then one day he was in the playground, when he saw Alice. She was scarcely moving and her beads were unnaturally still. There was a terrified expression on her face. Big Boy was in front of her, taunting her, while those pilot fish stood behind, and they were pushing her slowly towards an alley between two school buildings. He knew that something bad was going to happen.

He walked over there down the alley, and shoved Big Boy from behind.

He got the reaction he pretty much expected. All the hangers-on and other losers started laughing and looking at their hero to see what he was going to do. And this was the crucial bit. You don't hang around waiting for an answer if you don't want to get hurt. You've got surprise on your side. So Robbie took out the knife just as Big Boy was going into a narrowing-eyes routine, and before he could come out with anything clever, Robbie put out his hand and ran the blade over it ever so lightly so a thread of blood streaked over the ball of his palm. He watched the blood drip on to the ground. It was only like a paper cut, though Robbie noticed the tiny scar lines from where he'd had to pull this stunt before. The boy mountain couldn't take his eyes off his hand, so while he was staring at it Robbie put the knife right up under the boy's throat so he could feel its edge.

'Listen,' he hissed. 'Whatever your problem is, if you don't back off right now I'm going to take your throat out.'

He was looking into the widening eyes and he could see the fear there and he didn't want to waste it.

'And if we EVER –' he shouted this – 'have any more grief from you, you loser, and if you EVER even whisper a word to anyone about this, I – WILL – SHANK – YOU.' He spat the words out carefully so there could be no excuses for misunderstanding.

There was the sound of scrambling feet and in a few seconds the alley was clear of everyone except Alice and him.

'That worked,' he said, wiping the blade. Alice stared at him for a moment, then started to laugh.

And when she'd stopped laughing, she put her hand on his arm very gently and said, 'Thanks.'

That was how they had started to be real, proper friends. Robbie got a lot of filthy looks after that, and he was worried something was going to brew up, but it didn't, and they both got left alone. That's to say, they didn't make any new acquaintances or anything, they were kind of in a little leper colony all of their own, and Robbie sometimes saw Big Boy, whose real name was Elliot, looking at him in a peculiar, almost thoughtful way, but nothing happened.

She was very grounded, Alice, but she had spark as well. Sometimes she'd put her shoulders back and sometimes stretch out a leg and foot artfully as if she was a ballet dancer about to dance. That's when she was showing off a bit, aware of other people watching her. Quite a lot of the time she seemed not really to be listening to what other people were saying, she'd be off in her own dream world, and then when she tuned in and realized what they were saying she would turn to them in an instant; focused, questioning, doubting, hectoring. Sometimes she would just sit on one of the school benches, her knees crossed and an elbow resting on her thigh, carefully weaving together her beaded braids with the fingers of one hand, gazing into the middle distance as if trying to work things out. When she was in the right mood, which she often was with Robbie, she laughed so easily it was infectious, and those solemn eyes would flash with fire. Robbie wasn't even sure Alice *was* her proper name, but it was what she used and it suited her. Alice had opinions on everything, she was inquisitive; she had a mind like a silver fish flicking through the water. She had wisdom too, and seemed to understand things almost without having them explained to her. They used to talk and talk, they talked all the time. When Alice's mum and dad had split up, she chose to stay with her dad and they'd come to England, where he'd remarried. Alice liked her new mum, but she missed her home. Robbie thought he'd like to go there one day.

Alice didn't seem to have opened up to anyone about this stuff before, and of course he found himself telling her about his mum, which was hard because he hadn't talked about it to anyone, not properly, not even to Mags. Mags wasn't the only one with hiding places.

9

'HAVE YOU *seen* it?'

The trouble with Jess was, she squealed a lot. It was as if everything in her life had to be played at maximum volume. She was looking at Robbie from her chair and holding her earpieces out on either side of her head as if they had electrocuted her, and there was an expression of happy horror on her face.

The sisters, Jess and Lucy, hadn't been that much help to him. They were so close to their mother it was almost unhealthy, and he was sure they told her about everything he did. He was never quite sure what they thought about his dad; they could be flirtatious with him, but he'd seen them give him really filthy scowls behind his back, especially when he dared ask them to do something for him. They had the run of everything, and they knew it.

Lucy was the oldest and had GCSEs coming up.

She behaved as if she was standing to be an MP or something. She threw herself around the house like an underfed horse and often closed her eyes to show that no one could possibly understand her suffering, and when she was revising the house had to be absolutely silent. Especially Jess and her squealing.

Robbie and Jess had a sort of on/off secret alliance. She was younger than him and fascinated by what she saw as his outlaw past. Lucy was very suspicious, and every now and then she would swoop down and smother her younger sister with attention, as if to stop her being tainted by Robbie's company, and if there was one thing Jess loved it was attention. She was growing her black hair long and had put a red streak in it, and today was wearing a short red skirt and grey tights.

'I said have you seen it?' Her voice rose another octave. 'Don't walk off like that.'

'Yeah, it's wicked,' he said. 'Just what we needed.'

For the second time someone was suddenly pulling at his arm.

'Get off me, Jess.'

'No, really, Robbie, you've got to come and look, you've got to, it's huge. Mum and Alan are furious. I had to peel them off the ceiling.'

He sighed.

'Where are they, anyway?'

'Outside. Waiting for the police.'

His dad and Sheila were on the lawn, standing apart from each other and staring at the wall of the house. There was a hedge on the other side of the lawn with a big iron gate where the drive joined the road. There were mirrors everywhere so that if you were driving you could see what was coming round the corner, whatever direction you were coming from.

Sheila was hugging herself and smoking, which was something she only did when she was seriously upset. His dad was wearing that frightened expression again. Jess could hardly keep two feet on the ground.

Three letters, a metre high, in white paint. Tall and strong. They'd taken their time.

RUN, it said.

'Do you know anything about this, Robbie?' asked Sheila. He could hear the accusation in her voice.

'Why should I?'

'I didn't say did you do it, I just said did you know anything about it? Never mind. I'm sure the police will be very helpful.'

'Mum, don't be horrible to Robbie, that's really unfair,' said Jess, but Sheila put on a knowing expression that made Robbie want to hit her.

Jess linked her arm through his.

'How long's it been here?' he asked his dad.

'I think they may have done it in the night. Didn't you see it when you went out this morning?'

'No, I didn't come this way. What's it mean, then?'

'Oh, that's very obvious,' said Sheila. 'Someone doesn't want us living here.'

'Well, it's not me.'

'I didn't say it was. But there aren't that many candidates.'

'Mum,' warned Jess.

'I'd say there's a whole village of them,' said Robbie.

He knew who Sheila was referring to. The people who'd lived there before them. Mags's people. But he didn't believe that for a second. Mags wouldn't, her dad was a loser, her mum had moved on.

He gave his dad a look. Why wasn't he helping him out here?

'They even wiped their brush off on the wall afterwards,' said Jess.

'The scum,' said Sheila. 'The miserable, rotten, dirty scum.'

Under the letters were a few untidy white lines.

'Insult to injury.'

'Bloody, bloody nerve,' said Sheila.

The police arrived in a blue and yellow car. Robbie's skin itched with bad memories, and he didn't hang around.

Jess came into his room. She couldn't contain herself. Lucy was pretending to be above it all.

'She's being such an emo,' said Jess, her face a knot of irritation. 'So who do you think did it? The police seem to be a bit puzzled.'

'Like they care.'

'Do you think they don't?'

'We're outsiders.'

'Your dad isn't.'

'True.'

'Do you think he's happy being back?'

'I don't know, what do you think?'

'He's your dad, Robbie.'

'First off, I didn't think he was too fussed. But he's been getting into it, hasn't he? Spending time down at the Wheatsheaf.'

'Yeah,' said Jess. A foxy look came into her eyes. 'We noticed.'

Robbie knew what she meant, and he didn't say anything, because if Sheila and his dad weren't so loved up any more he couldn't exactly say he'd be losing sleep over it.

That was twice he had caught his dad with that expression on his face, though. There was something worrying him, and it wasn't Sheila.

'Dinner,' came the call from downstairs.

Lasagne. Again. She doled it out amid silence. It was a ritual, Robbie thought, equal portions carefully measured, salad to follow, everyone having to say how good it was because if they didn't, Sheila would. Lucy and Jess and Robbie's dad dutifully complied. Sheila eyed Robbie meaningfully.

Dad, why did you get us into this?

If he was going to be fair he'd admit Sheila could cook some lovely new things too, and she certainly didn't get any help from his dad.

But why would he want to be fair?

'What did the police say, Alan?' Lucy broke the silence.

'They didn't seem to be that interested.'

Robbie looked at Jess, which was a mistake.

'You two know something about it, then?' asked Lucy in a mean voice.

'What's the matter, Luce, someone got the jam out of your doughnut?'

'Robbie,' said his dad.

'What?'

'Don't be offensive.'

'I don't like her looking at me like that.'

'She didn't look at you.'

'Yes, she did.'

'Did you, Lucy? I'm sure you didn't. Robbie's just being sensitive. But did you?'

'It wasn't me looking at him, it was him looking at Jess.'

'Well, we were just talking about it,' said Jess. 'Robbie thinks the police won't be interested 'cos we're not local.'

'Robbie makes very free with his opinions, if you want my view,' said Sheila.

'So were they interested?'

'I'm sure it's not because of that, they've just got more important things to think about.'

'Oh, rubbish, Alan,' said Sheila. 'It's vandalism, sheer vandalism, and they'd better look into it sharpish or I'm going to be talking to their superiors.' Sheila seemed to think the police were like a department of Selfridges. 'I think I can give them a few pointers.'

'It's nothing to do with Mags.'

'Well, she did live here, Robbie,' said Jess.

'Yeah, right,' added her sister.

'So? Just 'cos she doesn't like something doesn't mean she's going to commit some atrocity over it. She's not like that.'

'We'll see,' said Sheila.

'Don't get her into trouble.'

'Robbie,' said his dad.

'She's my friend.'

'She's very strange,' said Sheila. 'Has she any friends apart from you, Robbie? She's quite a bit older, isn't she?'

'Loads of them.'

'Not many,' said Lucy.

'Does she have a boyfriend?'

'Used to,' answered Lucy.

'How come you're suddenly such an expert?' asked Robbie, his anger rising.

'Someone told me.'

'What were you talking to someone about her for?'

Lucy pulled in her chin so she looked like a stuffed frog.

Robbie pushed his plate away and got up. His face was flushed.

'Robbie!' said his dad, alarm bells ringing.

'No, Dad, listen. Especially you. It's this. I'm so sick of people telling me what I can do and what I can't, who I can be friends with and who I can't, and then trying to get them into trouble and sneaking and snooping around trying to find things out about them. She doesn't deserve it. I don't deserve it. Neither of us deserve it.'

He was hitting his fist hard against his thigh. Usually it helped him to concentrate. But he was agitated and it wasn't working. He was boiling up inside. He didn't seem to be able to see clearly.

There was silence, save for the beating of his fist. They were all looking at him.

Upstairs, the grandfather clock began to chime, pure, sweet notes. The tension held, and then dissolved.

'Eight o'clock,' said Sheila busily. 'Good. Time for some pudding. Give me your plates, everyone.' She cleared them away and came back from the kitchen with an apple crumble. 'Moving on,' she said. 'I thought that was rather good, didn't you?'

~

'I know what they'll be thinking,' said Mags.

'They'd better not see us.'

They were squinting in from the lane. The mirrors made them look as if they were surrounded by themselves.

'Can you see it?'

Mags was quiet. Maybe she was sympathizing with the message.

'It'll be some idiot from the Wheatsheaf. Coming back from a late one.'

'They'd have to go and get the paint first, though. It looks pretty deliberate to me.'

'Wait, though. Robbie?'

'Yeah?'

'See those white lines? The ones underneath the letters?'

'Uh huh.'

'Can you see what they are?'

'Where someone's wiped the brush.'

'I don't think so.'

'You've lost me.'

'Those two strokes on the left could be its hind legs, then there's two curving ones that could be its body, then two more long ones over the top are like its ears . . .'

A white hare, running.

'No wonder your dad was scared.'

'You think he saw it?'

Mags shrugged.

'So was he scared, 'cos it's really happening, or 'cos he thinks it's happening?'

Mags laughed. 'Like I said, Robbie, believe what you want. Whatever makes you happy. But don't say I didn't tell you.'

She jumped down from the bank behind the hedge into the road. The movement ricocheted in the mirrors.

'Now let's get out of here before they see me.'

IO

HIS DAD managed to get the white paint off the wall and spent even more time at the Wheatsheaf, trying to pick up clues, he claimed, but Robbie didn't think any of them were fooled by that. Least of all Sheila, whose temper got worse and worse as the weather hotted up and summer settled in.

So he took the advice on the wall. Someone had to.

He ran.

He ran through the fields and the woods, along the lanes, by the rivers and over the hills. The hedges were packed with campion and Queen Anne's lace bowing and dancing in the western winds, and the woods were dark and cool, the chestnut leaves big and friendly, dropping down like fat green fingers. He was beginning to learn where everything was, how the roads connected, where the rivers met, which hills neighboured each other. He went out after school and didn't get lost so easily, and it was better to run then because the air was cooler and clearer and cleaner.

Sometimes Alice came over at the weekend. Mags loved her and so did Sheila. Robbie thought it gave Sheila's middle-class conscience a thrill to have a black kid in the house, and it annoyed him because he didn't want her to like his friends, but she calmed down a bit when Alice was around and started showing off how cosmopolitan she was and how she'd been to lots of different countries. She'd been a great traveller in her time, Robbie had to give her that. And he couldn't help it, but when Sheila relaxed he did stop wanting to burn the house to the ground for a bit, and that had to be a good thing.

'Isn't it interesting,' she said, one day after Alice had left, 'how none of us really belong here? Except your dad, of course, Robbie,' she added. So he's just my dad now, is he? Robbie thought. Well, okay. And she's feeling a bit excluded. Well, okay too. 'Speaking of whom,' she went on, 'Robbie, can you go and fetch him? He's refusing to pick up on his phone and I know exactly where he is.'

'Wheatsheaf?'

'Yes.'

'His second home.'

'Many a true word,' said Sheila. 'Let's hope it doesn't become his only home.'

~

As Robbie was walking past the village store Mags came out.

'I'm going to spring Dad from the pub,' he said. 'You coming? And could you get your dad to bring his tractor and some chains? I'll probably need some help.'

'I'm not going in there,' she replied.

'Come on, Mags, it's not far, haven't seen you for a bit.'

She looked away.

'You go,' she said. 'Have a nice time.'

'Something wrong?'

'I don't like the people who drink there.'

'Well, can you wait? I'll put the fear of Sheila into him, that should do it.'

'I haven't got all day.'

'Why don't you go and sit in the churchyard? Bit shadier there.' She was wearing wellies and her green jacket; no wonder she was unhappy in that heat, it was burning hot and had been all week. There was a thin film of perspiration on her forehead.

'Okay, but don't be long.'

Colecombe lay in a small valley. To Robbie, it was a place of uncertain mood, its home and shops clustering together for company along the road. It had a green in the middle and another at the far end, a long pond with a war memorial at one side, and a church called St Paul's standing halfway up the valley side. Sometimes it was a sunny, happy place, and sometimes it seemed to be brooding and ill at ease, dwelling upon its own secrets.

Winkling his dad out of the Wheatsheaf was never going to be the easiest job in the world. The trouble was, thought Robbie, he was going native. He must have been about twenty when he left, saying he'd never return, but he had an amazing memory for who lived where, and who they were related to, and what they did for a living, and who owned what, going back decades. He liked a gossip, and people seemed to like him, well, he could be a charmer when he wanted to be. Perhaps it was helping him to make sense of what had happened to him in his life too.

Robbie stood waiting for his dad, but the banter went on and on, and he noticed a bunch of guys in the corner who kept throwing glances his way. Two of them were obviously brothers – they had the same black curly hair that straggled down to their shoulders – one had bushier eyebrows and a long nose and kind of pretty lips and a dimple. The other one, younger, was not so Johnny Depp, but Robbie could tell they both fancied themselves. They'd got leathers on that must have cost a packet.

'All right, coming,' said his dad. Sunny smiles all round, but not, Robbie noticed, in the direction of his new friends.

'Who are the top boys, then?' Robbie asked.

'Uh?' He'd obviously had a few.

'The retards in the corner.'

His dad was doing up his jacket and he turned in the direction Robbie was facing, then looked as if he wished he hadn't.

'Let's go,' he said.

'Come on, Dad,' Robbie said outside. 'Who are they? They didn't like me much.'

'Don't go near them, mate. They're not very pleasant.'

'I could guess that.'

'Heartbreakers, those two. Runs in the family.'

He shook his head and started walking home, not even noticing that Robbie wasn't following.

The road up to the church was white and dusty. When Robbie got there, Mags was sitting on a bench in the shade of the big sycamores, her feet tucked under her, chin in her hand.

''S'up?'

She pulled a face and shrugged. 'Mum's being really irritating.'

Mags seemed to be permanently at war with her mum, who was always criticizing her clothes and the way she looked. She didn't glam herself up, Mags, but her mum always tried to be ten years younger than she actually was.

'Shall we go and look in the church?' He liked

churches; they made him feel calm, his anger and anxiety absorbed into that still echo of space. This church had a square tower rather than a spire, which his dad said made it Norman, and inside he could smell the quietness, how, for hundreds of years, people had gone there to get away from their lives.

'Not really my thing, churches.'

'Why not?'

She glanced over to where the church sat serene, queenly among the trees. That face again, turned-down mouth, wrinkle of the nose.

'My aunt's a big believer. She's so not like Mum, she thinks Mum's a terrible sinner. She always made me come here on Sundays, forced me to, Mum and Dad just let her. I think they thought it was good for me.'

'When did you stop?'

'I was about twelve. I was going to be confirmed. I suddenly didn't want to go through with it. It's not for me, Robbie. Not for me.'

'Come on.'

Her eyes fixed on him, set hard.

'You don't get it, do you? Some things work one way, some things work another. This is not my way.' Then she smiled unexpectedly. 'But as it's for you.'

Inside, Mags cast looks around her nervously, but eventually she relaxed. She knew her way around the church, that was for sure. She knew all the saints in the stained glass and their stories. She told Robbie about the colours of the cloths over the altar and what they meant. She ran her hand over the plain dark wood of the pulpit, gently as if it might be hot, then opened the door to the vestry.

In the corner of the room the priest's robes hung on a long mirror, angled in a wooden frame. And there was Mags, illuminated by the light breaking through the window, pale and white like a ghost, but crossed with a stripe of fiery redness from the stained glass above and reflected in the mirror against the cool dark. With a surprising strange solemnity Robbie thought, this is how I shall always remember her.

'I'm going to read,' she said. Maybe her childhood was reclaiming her. Maybe that's what she was afraid of.

She went to the pulpit and ran her fingers through the pages of the huge Bible, then stopped.

> 'To everything there is a season, and a time to every purpose under heaven . . .'

Her voice was light and clear.

> 'A time to weep and a time to laugh, a time to mourn and a time to dance . . .'

She raised her hand, palm outwards. She looked as if she was blessing something, or pushing something away.

'*A time to embrace, and a time to refrain from embracing . . .*
A time to love . . .'

She peered up at the ceiling for a moment and twisted her head, trying to make something out.

'Oh, yes,' she said. 'Look, Robbie.' She pointed.

Above them was a wooden carving. Three hares running in a circle.

'I remember,' said Mags. 'In Dorset they're called the Tinners' Rabbits. Lots of churches have them. Only they're not rabbits, they're hares. Look at their ears.'

It was a kind of optical illusion, because there were only three ears in the carving, but each hare seemed to have two.

'I wonder what it means.'

'The Trinity,' said Mags. 'Father, Son and Holy Ghost. "A three-fold chord is not quickly broken." That's one of my aunt's favourites. It's like the feeding of the five thousand. There are more ears to go round than there really are.'

'The holy hares,' said Robbie.

'The holy hares,' repeated Mags.

'They get everywhere, don't they?'

'They do. That's their nature. Those beautiful creatures.'

'Beautiful.' He nodded. 'Like your reading.'

She smiled.

'I always loved those words.'

~

Jess was sitting on his bed, trying her best to annoy him and stop him doing his homework.

'So,' she said, hugging her knees. 'You like Alice? Floats your boat, does she?'

'Not the way you mean.'

She frowned. 'Mags?'

'Definitely no.'

'Why do you hang out with them?'

'Because I want to. You don't get anything, do you?'

'They're losers.'

'Whatever.'

They stared at each other. Then Jess put a big false smile on her face and batted her eyelashes at him.

'Anyway, me and Dad were in the Wheatsheaf and there were these chumps in there who really fancied themselves and Dad said not to go near them. Know what that's about?'

'Might be the Strickland brothers. Tommy's the older one, Billy's the younger. They're always in there. I've heard Luce talk about them. Really fit? Leathers?'

'That's them. How does Luce know about them? She doesn't go near the place.'

'She gets all that stuff from Mrs Allardyce.'

'She doesn't go near the place, either.'

'No, but she knows everything. Nothing moves

here without Mrs A knowing about it. And she and Luce are like that.'

'Yeah, she's always there, isn't she? Must be how she knows Mags doesn't have a boyfriend.'

Jess gave him a look. 'You were so angry.'

'Anyway, the Stricklands. What do we know about them?'

'They've got a farm over there somewhere.' She waved her arm.

'Could you be a bit less blonde and fill in the detail, Jess?'

'I'm not blonde. Don't be so rude. I'm the least blonde person you know.'

'Sorry.'

'You want to be mates with them? I think your dad might be right about that.'

'Just curious.'

'It's at the end of that lane with the funny name.'

'That's not much help.'

'Dancing Lane. Brading Wood Farm, I think it's called.'

The place Mags wouldn't talk about, where the Land Rover was going.

'Thanks. And Jess?'

'Yes?'

'You may leave my room, now, thank you. I have all this lovely homework to do.'

I I

ROBBIE COULDN'T get the Strickland brothers out of his head. It was because of Mags, of course it was. He wanted to know what she'd got to do with them. So it was not that long before he was running through the wood near where they lived. Brading Wood, he supposed.

It was a warm Sunday afternoon. He hadn't seen Mags for a while, but he'd been dreaming and it had been bringing him down a bit. In his dreams Mum was smiling at him, but that just made it worse. Sometimes she was sitting by his bed, not saying anything. Or walking down a street on her own, looking for something or someone, maybe him. Or staring out of a window, the light sharp, white, intense on her face. Or sitting in her chair, reading, slowly turning pages. And sometimes she was pulling at something, something on the wall, and she didn't get hold of it properly. Then when she did, it flew through the air in a blur, and he couldn't make it out. Maybe it was a bird or a big moth; there was a lot of fluttering and flapping going on. He was thinking about her lots right now.

The path through the wood was hard to follow, and it wasn't long before he didn't know where he was. So far it had been okay because the trees were spaced evenly. There were lots of oaks, and some beeches, the tall ones with smooth trunks that go way up before the branches start. His mum's favourite tree.

The trees fell away and he came to a clearing. The ground shelved into a shallow hollow like a big empty swimming pool, full of brown twisted dry leaves from last autumn. It felt like the sort of place to stop and rest, for lying on his back and looking up at the sky through the beech leaves and the oak leaves and daydreaming about things, about Mum, about life so far, about friends, about the future, even though Robbie couldn't even begin to imagine that.

So that's what he did, stretching out on the bank of the hollow, his soul emptying into the generous earth beneath and the calm woods around and the distant sky.

Then, like a burst of flame inside, a feeling came to him, a realization.

As the shock went through him, he sat bolt upright. Aware.

Something had happened here. The quiet was not real quiet, it was different. He didn't know what it was, but soon he was thinking, it's sad, so sad, the silence is full of it, this wasn't the good place he'd thought it was. This was a place of anger and hatred and unhappiness.

The leaves, the earth, the trees were full of it too, and he felt as if he was inside a moment, but he didn't know when or what that moment was.

He got up and walked further into the hollow, leaves deep and dragging at his ankles, and up the other side. Tied to an oak about ten metres away were some old sticks. As he got closer he saw they were the stems of flowers, some with the heads still on them, most without. They had been left the way people leave flowers by the road when there's been an accident and someone's died. He backed away.

But however hard he tried he couldn't run, he couldn't even walk fast. He felt as though he was wading through a marsh, though nothing had changed around him, the leaves were still dry and rustling. It was as if his body was no longer his own, and he knew it would be hard to escape the hollow. It was holding on to him, this fierce sadness he could feel all around beginning to work its way into his head.

And then he had to look back. He couldn't help himself.

A body was hanging from a branch of the oak where the bunches of flowers were. It was a girl, a girl with long blonde hair wearing a white dress.

He shut his eyes. It made no difference.

She was still there. He could still see her.

Still, still.

She was suddenly closer, her head on one side, the rope biting into her neck.

Then her eyes opened, deep blue, staring directly into his.

He wanted to move, but he couldn't. He wanted to speak, he wanted to run, run very fast, the fastest he'd ever run, but he couldn't.

Terror rose in waves, and there were other feelings, not his, he didn't know them or where they came from.

He felt as if he was going to crack into pieces. He felt as if those pieces would fly apart, to the opposite ends of the universe.

Then he'd have peace.

Tears were on her cheeks, and on his.

Nothing moved.

He was lying in the leaves, nearly buried.

She had gone. And he could run now.

Away from here, down the path, any path. He had to get somewhere, find someone. Past trees, ditches, hills, bracken, round a shoulder of hill to a road and a gate and then up the road between high hedges full of flowers, pink and white.

On and on, pounding the earth.

Another gate. A farm.

Their farm.

Where he knew he was meant to come, but now he was here, he didn't know why or what to do. As he leaned, sobbing, over the gate, whether from running or something else, he wasn't sure, except he felt that he'd been compelled to run this way and only now had that moment abandoned him.

Dogs started to bark. They didn't sound happy.

Dogs.

The sound brought him back to his senses.

It was late. He was shaking. Some kind of out of body experience, was that what it had been? He could feel himself returning, a bit shy and a bit bruised and a bit resentful at being left behind, as if he was saying to himself, 'What was that all about? Where'd you go, Robbie?'

The Alsatians were coming along the drive to the gate, making a ferocious row. The drive went into a yard past some buildings packed with hay on one side and a barn with its doors open. He could see an old tractor and a Land Rover inside. On the other side of the yard was a farmhouse, its bricks glowing orange in the light of the sinking sun. Someone was coming out of the front door with a shotgun under his arm.

'Hey!'

He was too wrecked to respond. His chest was still heaving.

'What are you doing here?' the figure shouted.

He was walking towards Robbie and straightening his gun.

'I'm lost.'

'Well, stop leaning on the gate for a start. Go on, get out of here.'

He was close, his eyes squinting in the sun, narrow like razor blades. His younger brother had come out of the front door too, and was standing, hands on his hips, watching.

'Sorry, mister.'

Tommy Strickland looked back at his brother, then at Robbie.

'You're Maggie Carr's toerag little friend, aren't you?'

'Yeah, I know her.'

'A bit more than that, mate. You're always hanging round her.'

'She's all right.'

He sneered. 'All right?'

'I mean, she's a friend, like you said.'

'You're not from round here, are you?'

What are they like? thought Robbie. People were always saying that to him, it was like the gangs back home, except they just knew he wasn't from their manor and he knew what to expect.

'If I ever see you with Mags, I'll kill you, mate. You stay away from her, right?' He spat. A big gob landed at Robbie's feet. Charming.

'We're watching you. Now go on. Run.' He shifted the gun in his arms.

You've got to be practical.

He walked, though. He didn't run.

12

IT WAS dark by the time Robbie got back, and Sheila was cooking. He texted Mags to say he needed to see her. He had a feeling she would know something. About the girl in the wood, about the Stricklands.

Jess came out of the kitchen and gave him her look. 'Problems?'

'Don't worry, you're not in trouble,' she said. 'Like, I mean, *you're* not in trouble.'

'I wouldn't say that.'

'Why, what's happened?'

'Never mind. What are we eating?'

'Salmon. With that sauce you like.'

'Great.'

'If Sheila doesn't throw it at your dad first.'

'Why?'

'They're having a domestic,' she said slowly, emphasizing each word.

'What about?'

'Oh, you know, late back from the pub. That's how it started, anyway.'

Robbie went into the sitting room, which seemed to be full of Lucy, draped over a sofa, watching TV. He thought he might see if he could find a map with Brading Wood Farm on it. His dad had a collection of all the big Ordnance Survey maps for everywhere local. He liked to sit with them and plan long walks for him and Sheila, which they didn't actually very often go on, but sometimes they did. It was as if his dad loved the planning as much as the walking, or just loved looking at maps and working out where things were and how they related to each other, running his finger over the contour lines and the red and yellow lines and the green woodlands.

'Hi, Luce.'

'Oh, hi, Robbie. Where've you been?'

'Just out running.'

'You do lots of running, Robbie.'

'You're right, I do.'

He hung around, hoping maybe she'd go, but she didn't. So he went to his room to think. Mags had texted, 'What's the matter?' so he texted back, 'Scared.'

Dinner was the usual nightmare, though he wasn't concentrating much. Somewhere inside he was still shaking.

'You okay Robbie?' asked Jess.

'You're right, Jess, he doesn't look very well. You're a bit pale,' fussed Sheila.

'Robbie?' questioned his dad, as if Sheila's fussing allowed him to fuss too.

'I'm fine. I was running, maybe ran too far too fast.'

'Running away?' asked Lucy.

He really didn't like that girl.

'No. I don't run away from things.'

There were candles burning on the table. Sheila liked to create an atmosphere, and Jess had a habit of flicking her finger over a flame to test the heat.

'I wish you wouldn't do that,' said Sheila.

Jess ignored her.

'And please don't use your fork when your elbow's on the table, Robbie, it's very ugly.'

'Dad does it.'

'No, I don't.'

'Yes, you do,' said Jess.

Dad looked flustered, and combed his fingers through his hair. He threw a conspiratorial glance at Robbie, his eyes glinting in the candlelight. Robbie felt a glow of happiness. His dad's gaze returned to rest on the plate in front of him.

'This is delicious,' he said.

'Good, good,' said Sheila.

'Did you have an interesting time in the pub, Alan?' asked Lucy, stirring things up.

'Some nice people in.'

'What, like the Stricklands? They're not nice,' remarked Jess.

'They've done no harm to me.'

'They haven't had the opportunity.'

'Don't give them one,' said Lucy.

'Don't worry, I'm not an idiot.'

'Who are these people?' asked Sheila.

'The Strickland brothers. Two of them,' his dad explained. 'Very old family, been farming here for centuries, three farms they've got, I think. They've always had a reputation.'

'They don't sound very attractive,' said Sheila.

'Oh, they're attractive,' said his dad. 'Especially the older one, in this current generation. That's the problem.'

'Heartbreakers, you said, Dad,' said Robbie, and his dad nodded.

'Your Mags went out with the younger one. Billy.'

'That girl has no taste,' said Lucy. Robbie was too amazed to say anything.

'And she had a friend, Fran, who was crazy about Tommy, the older one. They were quite a foursome, apparently, kind of Bonnie and Clyde squared.'

'Presumably they didn't end up the same way?'

'Sadly, in a way, one of them did. Something went wrong, and Mags's friend committed suicide. Typical Strickland story. Lady killers. Literally, in this case. Mags was pretty bruised herself, I'm told. In more ways than one. That's what they're like.'

'Do they always survive?'

'No, not always. They're not a lucky family. Their father shot himself, years ago.'

'What happened?' asked Jess.

'His wife found him in one of the barns. There were rumours they'd been quarrelling, so some people think she had a hand in it, but no one would dare accuse Eliza Strickland of anything. She's a terror.'

'I've met her,' said Sheila. 'I thought she was rather splendid.'

'Me too, often,' returned his dad. 'Makes my blood freeze.'

'You're just afraid of strong women, Alan,' said Sheila. Robbie could have sworn she was simpering.

'When did you meet her?' Robbie asked.

'She's very involved with the fair.'

'Oh god, the fair,' said his dad. 'When is it?'

'Next Saturday. I'm manning the second-hand bookstall,' said Sheila.

'We know, Mum,' said Jess. 'You've not stopped talking about it for months.'

'I'm going to be giving our bookshelves a good going over,' she said. 'I'm sure there's plenty we can get rid of. There are all those Mills and Boons of your aunt's, Alan, I don't know why you've kept them.'

'Sentiment,' said Lucy.

'And your old books from uni.'

'I can't imagine our neighbours will want books on conveyancing,' said his dad.

'Well, what about all your natural history, then? You never look at it.'

'I can't imagine they'd want that, either. Coals to Newcastle.'

'No, if you live in the countryside you're bound to want books on the natural world.'

'But they know everything they need to know. Anyway, I want to keep them.'

'Suit yourself. I'm going to have those Jeffrey Archers, though.'

His dad raised his eyes and said nothing.

'That really is unfair on the neighbours,' said Jess.

Robbie had a text from Mags. 'See you at bridge in 10.'

'I'm going out,' he said.

'You are not,' returned his dad.

'There's strawberries,' said Sheila.

He texted Mags back. 'Make it 20.'

As usual, Mags was sitting on one of the lower railings with her arms folded on the top one and her legs hanging over the water.

'What's happening, little bro?'

Robbie told her about what had happened in the woods and afterwards, and as he talked she began to stare intently at him and a confused, unhappy look came over her face. Then she stood up.

'Have you said anything to anyone?'

'No, why?'

'Don't. That's the first thing. Don't tell *anyone*.' She ground the last word out of her mouth like a kind of snarl.

Here we go again, he thought.

'Okay, sorry, Mags, I didn't know.'

She began walking, up the hill, out of the village, shoulders hunched, hands deep in the pockets of her jeans. Robbie found himself skipping just to keep pace with her.

After a bit they came to the green and sat down on a bench. Robbie bit his lip and tried to think what to say, and Mags pulled her knees up under her chin and wrapped her arms round her legs.

'Come on, Mags,' he said awkwardly.

There was a little choking sound, and he looked at her to see her cheeks were wet.

He tried to put his arms around her, but she wrenched herself free.

'Please,' she said. 'Leave me alone.'

He thought, it's me that's having visions and probably going crazy. I'm the one who needs help. It all means something to Mags, whatever it is, and she won't tell me about it. As per usual.

He didn't believe in it, anyway.

Didn't believe in any of it.

Weird country stuff.

Okay.

He might as well go home.

'Dad,' he said when he got back. 'How did Mags's friend die?'

His dad was doing some late-night washing up, and held a glass up to the light to see if it was clean.

'I'm afraid the poor girl hanged herself.'

'In those woods, over towards the Stricklands' farm?'

'Why do you ask?'

'Just something someone was saying.'

'An affair of the heart, as I said. Such things are best forgotten, as a whole.'

He went on polishing the glass.

13

WHEN ROBBIE dreamed of his mum he would wake up and feel as if he could hardly get out of bed. But tonight he was glad to see her and he felt sad, but not bad sad.

They were walking through rooms full of books. And, dreams being what they are, sometimes the books were there and sometimes they weren't. His mum's face was sharp and close and clear, he wanted to kiss her and he couldn't, but she was still smiling at him, like she used to before she got ill. There was light everywhere, and someone singing a tune that didn't seem to fit.

As they walked past the shelves, his mum put out her hand and books cascaded from them. As they fell they opened their pages and fluttered like wounded birds. They walked through room after room, and the books clustered in agitation around their feet.

Then Robbie looked down to see the books had become rushing water rising around them, but his mum was still smiling and holding his hand. There was a door ahead, and they were trying to reach it, though they weren't getting there however hard they tried.

He was beginning to panic, when the door opened and they were in a room he recognized. It was the room downstairs with the bookcases, the books all in place, and among them his dad's maps, one of which lay open on the table. He and his mum were poring over it, and he could see everything on it in detail as if he was looking through a magnifying glass. Dancing Lane. Brading Wood Farm. His mum was saying something, but he couldn't catch her words. Deep in the house the grandfather clock chimed.

Then they were in the wood, but his mum had disappeared and the hanging girl was there, only her eyes were open and sparkling and she was laughing. Together they watched a white hare running through the trees. Sometimes they could see her and sometimes they couldn't. She wasn't running away or towards them but round them, always to the left, like Mags had said when they were watching the hares in the field. Anti-clockwise, against the sun. Trouble coming. The girl raised her hand and the hare changed direction and ran down the hill towards Dancing Lane and the Stricklands' farm.

~

Sheila was excited about her stall. By now there were piles of books all over the house and not so many left on the shelves. Every day when Robbie got back from school there were more piles, more shelves depleted.

So when the day came, there was Robbie with Sheila, in a big white tent that was too hot, selling old paperbacks to the locals. He couldn't imagine why he'd agreed to help, but it was only for a while. There were lots of other white tents spread over a field that had a stream running round it, and there was a high ridge on the other side of the stream, quite cliffy, so it was all like some kind of secret place. Grey clouds were sitting on the other side of the hills, looking as though they meant business, and the heat was making his skin feel clammy. People from the surrounding villages had come, and it was only eleven o'clock but he could see Mags's dad shuffling about looking as though he'd already been on the cider.

'Everything fifty pence,' Robbie shouted, holding the books up. 'Dick Francis, fifty pence. Jilly Cooper, fifty pence. Sidney Sheldon, fifty pence. John Grisham, fifty pence.' Selling shedloads, he was. He was quite enjoying himself.

'How are you, Robbie? Nice to see you getting involved.'

'Thank you, Mrs Allardyce, d'you fancy some books? Danielle Steele for you? Fifty pence each, or I can give you five for two pounds.' And don't patronize me.

'No special promotions, Robbie,' said Sheila. 'Sorry, Mrs Allardyce. All for a good cause, you know.'

Robbie frowned. Special promotions? What did she think this was, Tesco?

'That's all right. I think I can stretch to two pounds fifty. Trouble is, I can't read Danielle Steele.'

'Don't worry, there's plenty of other junk here.'

'*Robbie*,' said Sheila.

'And what are you reading now, Robbie?'

'*Catch 22*.' He was holding up a Jilly Cooper. 'All books fifty pence each.'

'That's rather precocious of you.'

'Fifty pence each. Doing my best, Mrs Allardyce. Pretty impressive for a fourteen-year-old, don't you think?'

'Would you like to come over to visit us again soon? Tea next Saturday?'

'What, with Lucy?'

'Well, it would be nice to see you on your own, you know. We've been meaning to ask you for ages. I hope you're beginning to settle in more now?'

'There's lots of romances we've got here, Mrs A. They might be for you. Fifty pence a book, everybody.'

'I'm sure he would like to come, Mrs Allardyce,' said Sheila hurriedly. 'Wouldn't you, Robbie?'

'Good, we'll see you then, then.'

Not what they seem, Mags had said. Something made him uneasy, something in the tone of Mrs Allardyce's voice, as if he was being taken for granted, as if they thought they could do what they wanted with him. Maybe Mags was right.

As for Mags, she was just outside the tent. Most of her was hidden by a flap of canvas, but underneath it he spied her faded blue Converses.

'I'll be back,' he said to Sheila.

'Don't go, Robbie, you're doing a great job.' There was a pleading note in her voice.

'Honest, I will,' he said over his shoulder.

'Robbie, I need your help.'

'Won't be long.'

Mags was talking to his dad. He was in his shirtsleeves, and she was wearing a plain white t-shirt. Robbie heard her saying something about the beer tent. There was a worried look on her face.

'Sheila's let me go,' he said. 'So what's to do here?'

'Barbecues,' said his dad. 'Or rather BBQs. There's a coconut shy. Or you might try the plant stall, you know, make a contribution to the garden. Best dog competition, raffle, rubber duck race over there by the stream, and they'll be judging the woolliest sheep in about an hour.'

'Beer tent?' Robbie asked lightly.

'No,' his dad and Mags said together quickly.

The clouds were overhead now, almost black, and everything around sounded muffled. Thunder rolled like marbles in a shoebox.

'The dogs are cute,' said Mags.

'I like the rubber ducks,' said his dad.

'Rubber ducks, then the dogs,' Robbie said, deciding. 'How do you race a rubber duck, anyway?'

It turned out you raced a rubber duck by picking a number out of a hat. Then a box of yellow ducks got tipped into the water and floated all the way down the long loop of the stream. There must have been hundreds of them, and the one with Robbie's number on it was a lazy little waster that made exactly zero effort. His dad got terribly worked up, yelling at it as if it was in the Grand National.

'Go on, Number Seventy-two! Go on, Number Seventy-two! What are you *doing*? Get into the faster water, that's it!' Mags thought it was hilarious.

'You and Dad were being a bit cosy,' Robbie remarked, halfway round, feeling possessive of both of them.

'He's all right. A bit sad about things, I think.'

'I thought he reckoned you had something to do with that paint.'

'No, he was being really friendly.'

'Sheila does.'

'Yeah, she doesn't like me. But your dad's okay.'

'Mags?' Robbie asked.

She wasn't listening; she was too busy laughing at his dad.

'Mags.' He pulled at her t-shirt. 'Mags, I need some answers.'

'Not now, Robbie.' She was running after his dad.

'MAGS.'

Everything went quiet, and everyone turned to look at him. Mags stopped. He could tell she was angry.

'I'm sorry, Mags, it's just—'

'I'm sorry too, Robbie.'

'What did I see in those woods? I can't sleep at night.'

'Does she come back to you?'

'No, but I can't stop thinking about it. It's Fran, isn't it? Am I right? Something to do with your friend.' She looked startled. 'Dad told us the story.'

There was a buzz of voices around them again.

'And you know, don't you?' Robbie went on. Mags had her arms folded, as if she was wondering what to do with him. 'Don't you?'

'Not in front of all these people.'

'Well, where, then? You're always putting me off, you're never telling me. All that stuff about white hares—'

'Shut it, Robbie.'

'—And now this. But this is different. This is about me, and you know something, and I've got to know what it is. I mean, like, for a start, am I going crazy?'

'Do you feel like you are?'

'No. But maybe I am, I just don't know it. That's what happens, isn't it? People think they're totally normal when they've turned into a fruitloop.'

'You're not mad, Robbie.'

'That's worse, right? That means there's something happening and I don't know what it is, and I'm in it now, I'm part of it.'

'It looks that way.'

'So tell me.'

'It's not so easy, Robbie. I don't understand all of it. But it's been going on a long time. A long, long time. I should have known better, but I got involved, and now it's happening again. And I'm being bad, Robbie.'

'How?'

'I don't want them to know about her. I don't want them to find her.'

'Why's that bad?'

'Because of what will happen.'

'What *is* going to happen?'

Big drops of rain were beginning to fall and people started to run. Lightning forked over the hills.

'Okay, you guys, let's get under canvas.' His dad had arrived.

There wasn't much room in the beer tent. Everyone had piled in, laughing and excited. The roof thrummed to the rain. Robbie pulled at Mags's hand, but she wouldn't come in. She broke away and headed for one of the other tents.

'Right, everybody,' someone was shouting. 'Can you all hear me?' Everyone said yes in fake gloomy voices, and then they started laughing again at how funny they were. A little girl shouted no, and got another laugh of her own.

'I'm sure the rain won't last long, but while it does, why don't we have the raffle?' It was a tall thin woman who was just taking off her hat and rearranging her pile of grey hair. Her dark brown jacket was wet and glinted in the light. The earth was turning to mud outside, but it was dry in the tent, or dryish, given how much water people had brought in with them. There was, naturally, a huddle around the beer stall.

'Where's the tombola? Jacob, do you know where it is?'

'In the other tent,' someone shouted.

'Well, can someone please go and retrieve it?' Nobody moved. 'We can't have a raffle without the tombola, now, can we?' There was some asperity in her voice, as if she felt she was addressing a crowd of dim schoolchildren. 'Come on, someone, buck up.' In the end Robbie's dad took a plastic sheet from one of the tables, put it over his head and stepped out into the rain. Everyone cheered, and for a moment Robbie felt quite proud.

When his dad returned Mags was with him, and he was carrying a big brown wooden barrel. It was obvious she didn't want to be there.

'What's the matter?' Robbie asked.

'No room,' she said, which wasn't quite the reply he was looking for. She was completely drenched.

'She was standing in the rain,' his dad whispered to him. 'Mad.'

'Let me through, everybody.' It was the grey-haired woman, making her way through the crowd. She had a long face with beautiful lips, fine skin, sweeping eyebrows and penetrating eyes. She glanced carelessly at Robbie, but when she saw Mags her expression changed to one of anger and disdain. She looked as if she was going to say something, then swiftly turned away.

'Who's she?' Robbie asked Mags.

'Eliza Strickland.' She muttered the name as if someone was pulling the words out of her mouth, but there was a grudging respect in her voice.

She squatted down, looking at her shoes and hugging herself, trying to make herself as small as possible. Maybe Dad's right, thought Robbie. Maybe it's not me who's losing it.

His dad was turning the tombola. He seemed absurdly pleased with himself, especially since Eliza Strickland apparently made his blood freeze.

'A hundred and thirty-one on the blue.'

Mrs Strickland had pulled a blue ticket from the barrel and was holding it up.

'A hundred and thirty-one on the blue,' she repeated.

'That's me.'

Someone was waving the matching ticket. Robbie

strained to see. It was an old man wearing a moth-eaten cardigan.

'What have I won, then, Mrs Strickland?'

'I'm afraid the prizes are in the other tent, but I've got a list here so I can tell you what the spoils are. Let's see. First prize is a bottle of champagne, Mr Boswell.'

A big cheer went up. Someone near Robbie said John Boswell had never drunk champagne in his life.

'You'll have to show him how to open it.'

The winner mimed popping the cork and squinting through his glasses at the label.

'My favourite year!' he shouted.

'Number three on the red.'

'Yes!' It was Mags's mum, swinging her hips in her leather skirt as if she was in a girl band, grinning and nodding at everyone.

'A bottle of amontillado sherry.'

'Oh, how lovely.'

'Number fifty-seven on the red.'

Everyone looked at each other. No one was claiming.

Then someone stepped out from the crowd at the beer stall, and everyone started to groan.

'You can't give a prize to your own son!'

Robbie's friend from the farm came up and took his ticket with a smirk on his face. Robbie stepped back and almost fell over Mags, crouching behind him, holding herself tighter than ever. Outside it was still raining hard.

'Oh, can't I? You just watch!'

'I won it fair and square, didn't I?'

Mrs Strickland looked at her son fiercely as if she owned him, and when he looked at her, Robbie thought, you could tell he knew she was his number-one fan. Robbie felt shaky. His mum used to look at him like that. Didn't she? It was getting hard to remember. He was sure she'd looked at him like that.

The Strickland boy put his hands in the air like a politician, looked round at everyone, and saw Robbie.

He looked surprised, then grinned in a way that wasn't funny. He immediately started scanning the crowd, and Robbie knew it was for Mags, and understood why she was making herself inconspicuous. She must have seen him earlier, and that was why she hadn't wanted to come in.

As ever, there was only one way to deal with this. Robbie went straight up to him.

'Hello, Mr Strickland.'

'What's he won, then?' someone shouted.

His mother was looking at the prize list, pondering. Robbie could see her eyes were running up and down the paper, looking for the best one. Either that or he'd won a bottle of perfume. Suddenly she made up her mind.

'A day for two at the races,' she said.

Cool as a cucumber, thought Robbie.

'Brilliant, Mr Strickland,' he said. 'I'll come with

you. Bad Boy, ten to one on. Well Butters, three to two favourite.'

'That's the best prize,' said someone. They didn't sound happy.

'It's not the best prize,' said Mrs Strickland quickly.

It had to be close, though. Tommy Strickland was smirking, and his mother was looking at him lovingly again.

'That's a bit much,' Robbie heard someone saying.

'Got a problem with it, mate?' said Tommy.

'He's just pleased for you, Mr Strickland. Probably hoped he was getting that one himself. Aren't people selfish?'

Tommy swivelled.

'Where's Mags? You know what I said.'

'Haven't seen her all day, Mr Strickland.'

'She was around, I saw her.'

'Thought you'd been in here all day, Mr Strickland.'

'Don't give me that. I know she was around somewhere. Where is she?'

He was looking over people's heads towards the entrance. Robbie was thinking, these guys do think they own people. It's the way they are. Mothers own sons, sons own their lovers.

Robbie decided it was time to change the subject.

'The rain's nearly over,' he said. 'Can I buy you a beer? Not that it's allowed, of course. I can just give you the money and, you know, you can buy it yourself.'

But it was okay. Mags had gone.

'Number two hundred and eleven on the blue!'

'Over here!'

The Strickland boy looked him over one last time, lost interest and disappeared back into the throng.

Robbie went to find Mags. With the rain clearing, people were gingerly beginning to pick their way over the watery field.

There was a small figure near the exit gate, about a hundred metres away, running. The sun was out now, strong and bright, and Mags's t-shirt flared white. I didn't know she could run so fast, thought Robbie.

14

'I WANT you to help me in the garden.'

'What, just me, Dad? What about the girls?'

'It's man's work, Robbie,' said Jess. 'Anyway, we're going shopping with Mum.'

'You're going shopping, and I'm helping Dad?' But it was no use.

The garden had become his dad's new obsession. He was finally tackling the long grass, hoeing it first and then mowing it fine, and he was buying books about garden practice and design that were beginning to fill the gaps left in the bookshelves by Sheila's raids for her stall. The beds were being dug over and manure applied. His dad had found a favourite nursery where he bought car-bootfuls of new plants, and old ones were uprooted and thrown on the bonfire. Robbie thought this was probably a good thing, though he wasn't sure about the way his dad seemed to want him to share it all.

So he cut grass and dug holes in a border along the hedge by the road that his dad had cleared for roses, singing to himself to keep his spirits up. The roses were going to be underplanted by lots of other things, Robbie lost track of the names.

And it was hot. The clouds were low and grey and dry, and he felt stifled, as if his breath was being sucked out of him. He didn't say anything to his dad all day if he didn't have to, but his dad didn't seem to notice.

When the girls and Sheila got back they were carrying enormous carrier bags. They had been to a big shopping centre in Yeovil and were very cheerful about their purchases, the air suddenly full of their delight. Robbie kept mutinously silent, aware of their nervous, irritated glances, as if they were worried his sulking might lead to something worse.

'Dinner, Robbie,' called Sheila later.

'I'm not hungry,' he replied.

'You've got to eat something.'

'No, I don't. I don't have to.' Then he relented, but not entirely. 'Okay. But I'll have mine in the other room.'

Sheila opened her mouth to say something, then changed her mind.

Robbie sat eating quietly, trying not to seethe too much, listening to the murmur of voices next door. Jess was laughing.

Books were lying on the floor. Robbie remembered his dream about his mum, and the books flying off the shelves, and it came into his head to look at his dad's maps, to see if he could find the one they had been looking at, the one with the Strickland farm on it.

The maps were jammed so tight he had to pull hard to get them out, and when they did they came with a rush and a couple of books flew out with them, falling to the floor, just like in the dream.

One of them lay open, revealing something long and lean tucked into its pages. A letter. He stooped closer. The book was old, with faded colour photographs of animals and birds and their descriptions. He looked at the pages the letter had been nestling between. Then he picked the book up and read more closely.

'The mountain hare is reputed to moult three times a year, its coat changing from white to brown in the spring. Because the coat often takes on a blue hue when this happens it is also known as the blue hare. In winter the coat turns white again. As the seasons turn the hare is naturally vulnerable, for it may be white against the hillside or brown against the snow.'

Lepus timidus scoticus. The mountain or blue hare. It lives in Scotland and the Lake District and the Peak District.

Not from round here, then.

So was that all it was, a mountain hare, a long way from home, at the end of the season, fearful and lost?

He picked up the letter, and turned it over. 'For Robbie,' it said. He recognized the handwriting. His heart skipped a beat. For a moment or two he couldn't understand what was happening.

He opened it. He was right. It was from his mum.

Words flung themselves off the paper at him like a driving blizzard.

Five stood out.

'I know all about Sheila.'

And then he ran.

Into the dining room, where they were all sitting.

'Why did you hide it?'

His voice was quiet and controlled, masking his mounting fury.

Bewilderment crowded his dad's face, and he half-turned, as if he had been hit, his eyes fixed on the letter in Robbie's hand.

'Robbie, I . . .' he began.

'I said, why did you hide it?' Robbie's voice was louder now, steelier. 'Don't move,' he said to the others, as they began to push their chairs back from the table.

'I . . . wasn't sure what to do with it.' His dad's voice was faint, as if he was desperately searching for an answer. Then something in him changed. He turned back, and looked steadily at his son. 'Robbie, I'm sorry. Some things just aren't that easy to work out.'

'You were scared, weren't you? You're pathetic.

Just because you didn't know what she wrote, you hid it. I'm surprised you didn't burn it, though even you wouldn't do that. But it wasn't yours, was it? It was mine, mine from Mum when she knew she was dying.'

His dad stood. His face had turned crimson, though there was determination in him too. 'Please don't talk to me like that, Robbie. Life may not have turned out the way you wanted it to, but you're not the only one in this. Yes, I put that letter out of reach. Maybe I should have put it further out of reach, or maybe some part of me wanted you to find it. But we were going through enough, you and me both, and then what happened with you . . . I mean, what might that letter have sparked off in you? She asked me to give it to you, and with everything that was going on, I guess I forgot. And then I came across it again and remembered, but by then you were in no condition to be reading letters from your mum who was no longer there.'

'You *forgot*! This was for me. How could you *forget*?'

'Robbie, you're getting hysterical. You see, I was right. You've got to move on, you've got to put it all behind you.'

'Stop talking in clichés.'

'I'm not, I mean it. Look at what it's doing to you.'

'You don't understand.' Robbie shook his head slowly. 'You're so *stupid*.'

He turned, still clutching the letter, ran out of the house, and kept on running.

I'm not going back, he thought.

Never.

Running through the village, running up into the hills.

Leaving them, leaving everything behind.

Never going back.

15

IT'S WARM in here, thought Robbie. He didn't know what time it was, or how long he'd been there, or how long he'd stay. But at least it was warm.

The moon was full, big and bright and pearly and solid. Robbie liked full moons. He liked how they made him feel, whole and ready. Now it filled the chamber with light.

Earlier, he'd been sitting outside. Moonlight was everywhere, and the air was clear, and all the lights in the villages and towns on the Levels glittered. He couldn't see the stars so much because of the moonlight, you'd think they'd all fallen to earth, a little galaxy of orange streetlights sprinkled over the plain. Robbie wondered what was going on in those lives down there. Up on the beacon he didn't need anything; it was just him and the sky.

He had been thinking about Mags and how they'd

lain here, talking about their lives. This time he was thinking about who might have lived here, long ago. Families huddling together and digging up whatever it was they dug up. He wondered if it made them rich. No phones, no internet, no TVs, no stepmothers. Every day when they woke they'd be looking out over the whole world. And people would have died, and married, and lied and hidden things. So, much like our own world today, then, he thought. He could imagine himself as a TV archaeologist, saying that. His catchphrase. So, much like our own world today, then. People don't change. Things just happen faster.

He wasn't going back. Not after this. He didn't care what anyone said. He'd get Mags to buy him some food and blankets and things he needed. He'd stay here for the rest of his days, a hermit, the hermit of the beacon. People would come and see him for advice on how to live their lives better. Robbie, what do you do if your mum's dying of cancer? Robbie, what do you do if someone wants to beat you up for no reason? Robbie, what do you do if your dad's a total loser?

His head nodded and he drifted.

Suddenly he was awake. The chamber was still moonlit, but the moon had moved in the sky.

There was someone out there.

He could hear the whisper from the ribbon of road

far below. He hadn't noticed that before, there must have been a change in the air currents, carrying the faint sound towards him.

Someone was singing. He recognized that voice, that tune.

He listened hard. All his senses were tight like strings on a violin or a guitar. He didn't feel afraid. Where was it he had heard it before?

Now there were words. He couldn't catch them clearly yet.

Then he could.

Words he knew.

> *'The friendless one, the cat of the wood,*
> *The starer with wide eyes.'*

It was coming closer.

> *'The animal that all men scorn,*
> *The animal that no one dare name.'*

She was outside. And he knew who she was. He was beginning to understand.

There was a figure in the doorway, a little indistinct in a halo of moon brightness. She was coming in.

The cat of the wood. The starer with wide eyes.

She didn't seem to see him. She was looking for something, hands searching among the stones of the wall. She looked confused, then angry, and she was muttering softly to herself, 'Somewhere here, somewhere here.' She was wearing black tights and boots, a short grey skirt and a denim jacket. She was older than Robbie. Her hair shone in the moonlight, but he couldn't work the light out, there seemed to be more of it where she was. She stooped to a stone in the wall, which moved at her touch.

Then she stopped. She turned slowly and looked at Robbie. There was a peaceful look about her.

'I am Fleet.'

She was gone. He didn't even see her go, but he could hear her singing again outside, fuller and stronger than before.

> 'The animal that all men scorn,
> The animal that no one dare name.'

It was morning.

The sun was behind the hills, and the Levels were in shadow, covered by mist like layers of silk. It was cold.

He was stiff and hungry. He texted Mags to tell her where he was, hoping she would bring him something to eat. She had texted him twice already, she didn't seem surprised. She asked him what he wanted. A bowl of honeynut flakes, a bacon sandwich and a pint of orange juice should do the trick. She said he was mental.

The sun rose, the mists thinned, and the world lost its thoughtful look. Mags was taking her time.

Then he remembered.

He went back into the chamber. What had she been saying? *Somewhere here, somewhere here.*

The stones were set lengthways, each stacked on top of the other. They were packed together, holding in the earth behind. None of them seemed to want to move.

He was sliding his hand over them, along their tips, which poked out from the wall. *Somewhere here, somewhere here.*

He was really, really hungry now. Good one, Robbie, run away from home with no money, no clothes, no nothing. You're just a loser like Dad.

One of them turned.

He yelped in surprise.

He stared at the stone as if it had stung him. It had turned as easily as if it was on a hinge. And in a way, it kind of *was* on a hinge, because the stone rose to a peak, against the one on top of it, so he couldn't pull it out, but he could turn it. He could only move it a bit, not enough to make much of a difference, not even so it showed, unless you knew you were looking for something. It must have been like that since the wall was made.

Robbie looked closer, squinting behind the stone. There was a cavity there; he could just about get his hand in. He winced at the thought of feeling around in there. Who knew what was inside? Making his hand little and pushing hard he could squeeze it through the opening, scraping off skin. He felt something hard. Difficult to get out. If he took hold of it, his hand would widen into a fist, and he wouldn't be able to extract it. In the end he managed to tuck it under his fingertips and slide it out. He turned the stone back and looked at what he had found.

A memory stick.

He heard footsteps. A shadow fell on the stone doorway.

Was she back?

She couldn't be; she was only a dream.

But the stone had turned. So she was more than a dream.

He felt his stomach knotting.

What happened to you, cat of the wood, to make you do what you did? What's your story? I know you, don't I? I know what you're doing too. You and Mags.

'Hello?'

'Mags, I thought you were—'

'The police, I reckon,' she said, stepping through the door with a package in her right hand. 'The whole countryside's out looking for you, babe.'

'Yeah?'

'No. Police might have been called, but I haven't seen them. Can't say as I've been looking, though.' She started unwrapping the package. The smell nearly made him faint, he was so ravenous. It was a bacon roll. No, it was two of them. And the bacon was still warm.

Mags watched him scoff the butties, her face a mixture of fascination and revulsion. When the last crumb had disappeared, she spoke.

'So what's this all about, then?'

'I found a letter.'

'So?'

'It's from Mum.'

'Oh.'

Because he was thinking about the letter, he wasn't thinking about what he was doing, which was playing with the memory stick, turning it nervously over and over in his hand.

'What's that?' asked Mags.

'Something I found.'

'What, here?'

'Yeah.'

'All right.' She was going to say something, then she changed her mind. She was looking at it suspiciously.

'It's a memory stick,' she said.

'Yeah, I know.'

'Bit of a weird place to find it.'

'Yeah.'

'Was it, like, you know, lying around on the floor somewhere?'

'No.'

'Where, then?'

'What is this? I found it, that's all.'

'I'm just asking.' She sounded edgy, and Robbie wondered what was bothering her. For some reason, he didn't want to tell her the truth. She had been so guarded with him, and this was his.

'It was in my pocket.'

'You said you found it here.'

'Maybe someone dropped it.'

'You said it was in your pocket.'

'I think I might've picked it up without thinking about it and put it in my pocket, then sort of found it without realizing it was me who put it there in the first place.'

'You're winding me up, Robbie.'

'Maybe.'

'Well, stop it. Come on, I need to know.'

They stood, looking at each other, facing off. Mags put on her most winning smile. He shook his head deliberately.

'Don't try that, Mags. It's not going to work.' The smile disappeared.

'You're so aggravating,' she said. Then a sly look came into her eye. 'Okay, Robbie.' She stepped over to the wall and put out her hand. She rested it on a stone, then moved it from one to another, watching him. She smiled again, this time because she could see she was winning. It must have been written all over his face.

'Was it in here?'

She turned the stone, as if it was nothing, then swiftly bent down to peep into the empty cavity.

She knew.

He wasn't giving in.

'Yeah, I noticed that. Everyone must know about it. It's easy to find.'

'It's not easy, Robbie. You'd be surprised. Unless you know what you're looking for. These walls are thousands of years old.' She folded her arms. 'I'm telling you, Robbie. You have to know what you're doing and why you're doing it. No one turns this stone by accident.'

'Seemed easy to me.'

Her face lit up.

'So I'm right.'

At the same time she grabbed for the memory stick, but he was too quick.

'Hey, it's not yours.'

'You're right, it's not mine. Okay. But how did you know?'

'I'll tell you another time.'

The sly look came back.

'Can we share it?'

'Mags, you sound like you're six.'

She shrugged.

'So you know about this?'

She nodded.

'One of your hiding places, Mags?'

'Yeah. Someone else knew about it too.'

'Maybe it's theirs.'

'Maybe.'

'Could they have put it there?'

'That would be kind of hard.'

'Why?'

'She's dead.'

She was wandering towards the door, looking around the chamber, kicking the walls with her boots.

'Fran? You mean Fran? You said you used to come here with her.' Fran wanted it found, he thought.

Mags didn't reply. She was furious with herself. But she hadn't been in here since her friend died, he remembered. Apart from with him.

And maybe it wasn't there then.

'Robbie.'

'Yeah?'

'I've got to see what's on that memory stick.'

'Beg me.'

'What?'

'I mean it. Go on, beg me. You're always telling me what I can do and what I can't do. Now I've got something you want, and I'm not going to give it to you just 'cos you say so.'

'You creep.'

'And don't try anything on. I'm faster than you.'

'I'm between you and the door.'

'Stronger too.'

She started walking towards him.

'Come on, then.'

'You're crazy.'

'Know what? I think you're right. Either I'm crazy, or everyone else is. I see things. I keep seeing this girl. I think she's your friend. Fran. One time she's hanging, another she's singing. In the wood, in my dreams, outside here. I see the hare too, sometimes, in the distance, once in a dream. And I know it's all connected, and you won't tell me how, but I'm beginning to guess. What kind of a friend is that?'

'The kind who brings you bacon rolls when you've run away from home. The kind who maybe doesn't want to tell you things 'cos she doesn't want you involved, doesn't want you hurt.'

'Too late for that.' He waved the memory stick at her. 'Tell me something I don't know. Tell me about the white hare.'

'The hare's gone.'

'What do you mean?'

'What I said. I was keeping her. I caught her, and I was keeping her. I thought I could. No one's caught the white hare before, or kept her, but I did, and I kept her a while. I told you I was being bad. I was torn, Robbie.

Keeping her, maybe I was trying to be good. Why would I do that? After all that happened. Anyway, it's too late now. She's gone.'

'She ran away from me in my dream.'

'Where was she running?'

'The Strickland farm.'

'That's where she'll be going. I couldn't stop her. I did try, not as hard as I should have, I know. She has a name now, her own name.'

'Fleet.'

She nodded, looked tired, ran her hand through her hair.

'Seems like you know quite a bit already.'

There were voices outside. Men's. The first of the morning walkers.

'The memory stick, Robbie. Please.'

The voices had put her off her guard, though. It was easy. A rush, a push, a jump. He was out and running.

And no one was faster than him.

16

IT WAS a long way to Alice's, but he made it in the end.

He didn't want her parents to see him, so he waited up the road for her to come home from school, his hood over his head just in case. He had texted her to tell her where he was. His phone had been full of texts from everybody, he had deleted them all without bothering to read them. The battery was going, anyway.

He looked around him. Alice lived on an estate on the outskirts of Sherborne. Rows of new houses marched together like soldiers on parade. Sometimes a bus stopped at the end of the road and people got out and mingled, then disappeared home, leaving everything neat and regimental again.

Suddenly there was Alice coming towards him in her school uniform, eyes singing with excitement.

'You're in so much trouble,' she exclaimed. She gave him a big kiss. 'What are you doing here?'

'Coming to see you.'

'You're out of your mind.'

'Yeah, you're not the only one thinks that.'

'You can't come over to mine. My mum and dad will call the police. Or your dad.'

'Not sure which is worse.'

'Come on, what're you doing here?'

'Running away.'

'Really? And where are you going?'

She'd got a point.

'Need to find somewhere to hole up for a while.'

'"To hole up"? Robbie, your dad's in a total state. Your sisters are too. Jess called me. Oh, and the police came and pulled me out of school.'

'What for?'

'To see if I knew anything, 'cos Sheila told them we were friends.'

'She's all heart.'

'So what are you going to do?'

'Stay with you. Haven't you got a shed or something?'

She looked round conspiratorially. 'There's the garage. Dad's car's being serviced and there's some part they haven't got they've sent away for so he's not getting it back for at least a week.'

She took him to a row of garages painted a dull

blood colour. Some of them had cars outside on the tarmac, which sloped down to the road.

'Wait here,' she said. He watched the strings of red and blue beads bobbing in her hair as she ran, then he sat down on the warm ground. He was almost asleep by the time she was back.

'Sorry,' she said. 'Mum wouldn't stop talking, and it was hard to get the key without giving something away.' She twisted it in the lock, wrestled with the handle and pulled. Inside, the garage smelled of wet concrete. It was almost bare, except for some cupboards and some used paint tins stacked up on top of each other.

'Ta da!' sang Alice, pirouetting. A mattress was propped on its side, almost invisible against the dirty whitewash of the back wall. 'But, Robbie, am I going to get into trouble over you? Won't I be aiding and abetting or something? Isn't that what they call it?'

'I won't be staying long. And you'd go to the ends of the earth for me, you know you would.'

'Ends of the earth but not the Youth Court or whatever, that thing you went to.'

'No, it's not nice.' He pulled the mattress flat. It was spotted with black mould. 'I think maybe just the night.'

'All right, be fussy. Then where are you going?'

'Away.'

'You've got no idea, have you?'

'Yeah, I do.' Maybe London. Maybe look up his old friends. Would they want him back?

He was rapidly working out the downside of running away. He was so hungry again he could have eaten the mattress, mould and all. And people were walking past, the estate wasn't totally dead, it just looked it, so hiding wasn't going to be easy. And night was coming on.

Alice seemed to know what he was thinking.

'I can give you a few pounds if you want,' she said. 'It's all I've got. There's a chippy at the corner if you're desperate. I'll see what I can get you from home.'

'Can you leave the garage door open?'

'Nah, people'll think it's weird, they might take a look. I'll have to shut it. It won't lock from the inside, though, so I'll leave it unlocked. You can get out if you need to.'

'And anyone can get in if they want to.'

'Well, yeah.'

So he sat there in the dark, the light at the edges of the door beginning to fade. It seemed hours before she returned. She'd changed her clothes.

'I couldn't get away again,' she declared, after slamming the door down. She'd brought him a torch and some biscuits.

'Is that all? I'm going to die.'

'Mum knows her cupboards and the fridge inside out. She knows where every bean is. She'd notice. So don't be ungrateful.'

'I'm not. I'm just about to faint, that's all.'

'Here.' She pulled out a bottle of water.

'Won't she miss that, then?'

'No. Got it out of the bottles bag. Tap water.' She pulled off her jacket and then the sweater underneath. 'This is for you. It's usually at the bottom of my drawer. It's going to be cold in here.'

They lay on the mattress making shadows on the ceiling with the torch for a while, before Alice had to go.

'I'm pushing it, anyway. I'm not supposed to be out this late.'

After she'd left Robbie listened to the sounds from outside, trying not to lie on his side because the mattress smelled so bad.

Cars crawled past, then one swept up to the next-door garage, there was lots of banging and crashing and the car door slammed. He could hear some guys playing football in the dark, the ball slithering along the tarmac, the booms as it hit one of the garage doors they were using for a goal. Then some girls went by, talking loudly about some guy they fancied.

Robbie was thinking about that chippy. His stomach was howling for food.

He listened at the garage door to see if there was anything happening outside, then pushed it open a bit so he could slide underneath.

The chippy was a golden glow at the end of the road.

There were loads of people in there, and the smell was just too much. It seemed like forever before it was his turn, and suddenly there was a noise in his ear like the crowd at a football match, and he turned to find a policeman standing behind him. His radio had just burst into life. What with the smell and the wait and the shock and the worry Robbie must have swayed a bit, because he found the policeman looking down at him, his eyes narrowing.

'You all right, son?'

'Yeah, thanks. Just hungry.'

'You live round here, do you?'

'Yeah, over there. Well, just staying the night. Sleepover.'

'Where are you at school, then?'

Robbie told him.

The man behind the counter was looking impatient.

'Sorry,' Robbie said. 'Large chips, cod, large coke, please.'

'Aren't they feeding you at this sleepover, then?'

Robbie laughed as if he'd just heard the world's funniest joke. 'Yeah, I'm greedy, that's all. Guess I'm just a growing boy!'

'I'll have the same as him,' the policeman said.

'You greedy too, are yeh?' said the man.

'Hungry work, nicking people,' said the policeman, and turned looking for an audience. He got a big cheesy grin from Robbie, but everyone else looked bored.

'That's four-fifty.'

Robbie only had four.

'Oh, can you keep the Coke? What's that, then?'

'Three-ninety.'

'Yeah, got it.'

'You need some more pocket money, son.'

'Yeah, I do, you're so right, thanks.'

Then he was out, stuffing his face as he ran.

The salt made him thirsty, but he tried not to finish the water. He leaned back against the wall in the dark, feeling bloated.

So.

There was only one analysis of his situation, bleak, but simple. He'd got nothing and nowhere to go.

Some light was sneaking in at the edges of the door, mostly moonlight. It would last a few hours. The night stretched ahead.

He'd work it all out in the morning.

He was awake, at least he thought he was. Something had woken him. He had been drifting in and out of sleep, and he couldn't see a thing.

There it was again. Metal against metal. Just outside. Good thing I didn't reach for the torch, he thought.

What's out there?

There was no singing this time. Something scraped on the tarmac.

If he rolled over a few times he could make it to the door and maybe see though the gap between the door and the floor.

His gut felt tight and his heart was racing.

It had gone quiet.

Maybe it was the police. Maybe Alice had told them. Maybe her mum and dad had got it out of her, asking her where she'd been, they'd noticed the key was missing and then it wasn't, what were you doing in the garage, Alice?

He couldn't hear anything.

Maybe they'd gone.

Maybe they were waiting.

Waiting for what?

For him to make a move.

I'm going back to sleep, he decided, but of course he couldn't.

The silence and the darkness around him felt as if they'd come alive. They were listening, watching. It was almost as if they were about to talk to him.

What would they say, the silence and the darkness? They were cold and threatening, they would say cold, threatening things. Things about dying, about people who should be friends hating each other, about bad people always coming out on top.

He tried to sing to himself, but the words wouldn't come.

Something bumped on the tarmac outside.

Help.

No, wait, I know that noise, I've heard it before.

Slowly, slowly, he rolled towards the door.

Mustn't make a sound.

He reached the door and peered under it. Outside, a streetlight glared, and he could see the car outside the next-door garage. It was a Volvo. And he could see what he knew he would. The tyres had gone. Someone had jacked them. That's what the bump was, rubber on tarmac. He'd heard it, seen it, hundreds of times.

The thieves had vanished.

Relief flooded through him. He wanted to dance around the garage, hugging the darkness and silence and giving them kisses.

He could even have sworn the mattress smelled sweet.

He curled up.

Mags, that's it. Mags understands. One of her hiding places, she can hide me. Now Fleet's gone. She can hide me instead of Fleet.

Then what?

Then nothing. Something will happen.

Something will happen.

Something.

'*Robbie.*'

Oh, no.

Did he hear that? Did he hear someone calling him?

He was imagining it.

Sleep now.

There was that tightness in his gut again.

I need a doctor, that's what I need, he thought.

I've handled the silence and the dark and a bunch of tyre-jackers.

Anyway.

I imagined it.

See a doctor.

Go to sleep.

Mags. She'll sort it. She knows.

It's so dark. All the moonlight's gone now.

'*Robbie.*' There it came again.

No, no, he thought. I don't want this.

It was outside. It always started outside. He felt as if he was being invaded.

It was a girl's voice. Her voice. No singing.

What did she want?

He began to panic. What can I do? How can I stop her? How long will all this go on for?

The garage door trembled, as if a strong gust of wind had blown against it.

Then it began to open.

He couldn't move. He tried, but he couldn't. Was something holding him, or was he dreaming?

He couldn't see anything in the darkness of the

garage, but he could hear the door opening and there was light out there. Just enough, now, to see her, there was light about her, there was always light about her, and not just the streetlight.

He began to feel her pain again, like he had in the wood.

There she was. Black tights, boots, denim, long blonde hair. She was looking at him. For the first time he could sense her anger. Intense, vengeful.

What does she want?

Then something changed. She didn't look the same any more.

Who did she look like?

He thought, she looks, it's weird, she looks like Mum, when she was young, in pictures, how she used to be. I never saw her like that.

Something changed again, and again, over and over, and it was as if she had thousands of faces, passing like clouds across the moon on a windy night.

Then she was gone.

The door shut.

He was trembling. The sweat was cooling on his skin.

At least the pain had gone too.

He was left with the fear, biting into him.

And the silence and the darkness were laughing at him.

Told you so, they were saying.

He wanted to turn on the torch, but he couldn't in case anyone saw the light.

Not if he put it under his t-shirt, though. Just for a bit.

That was better. Much better.

He curled up round the torch. The light shone through, but softly, only for him.

17

ALICE SHOOK him awake. He sat up blearily and the torch fell to the floor. She leaned over and picked it up.

'You've used up all the battery, you muppet,' she exclaimed, annoyed. 'How'm I going to explain that, then?'

'Batteries run out. It's not that unusual.'

'You're going to get me in trouble, I know it.'

'You can get new ones.'

'And who's going to pay for them? Here, I've grabbed you a banana and some more water.'

'Wicked.'

A banana had never tasted so good.

'What are we going to do with you, Robbie?'

'I really don't know. Alice?'

'Uh huh?'

'Have you got a laptop?'

'Yes. Why?'

'I need one.'

'What for?'

'I've got something I need to see. It's a memory stick. I found it, and I know it's important, but I don't know what's on it.'

'I'll need my laptop for school, but you could use our computer, I suppose. It's risky, though.'

'Listen. You remember all that stuff I was telling you about Mags and the hare and the girl and these kind of visions I'm having? Well, it happened again last night. The garage door opened and there she was, and she kept changing, like she was lots of girls, lots of women I didn't recognize. Hundreds, thousands of them.'

He held her wrist, looking at her pleadingly.

She gave him a worried look, then made up her mind.

'Okay, here's the deal,' she said. 'I am going to get you a key to our house. Mum's going out, but leave it till eleven, just in case.' She told him how the alarm worked. 'So don't mess up, Robbie boy, or I'm in a lot of trouble.'

A few hours later and he was in the house. There were photographs on the wall and on the shelves, Alice and her dad, Alice and her mum, Alice and her mum and dad, all of them together.

He found the computer, switched it on and put in the memory stick.

Out of nowhere, there was someone on the screen,

scruffy and fluffy and blonde and laughing. It was Mags, Mags as he'd never seen her before, she was so happy. She kept waving at the camera, then doubling up with laughter. The camera was moving, he could hear whoever was holding it was laughing too.

They were sitting outside somewhere, the sun was shining, and there was a house in the background. It could be ours, thought Robbie. Whoever was holding the camera got up, bringing more of the house into view, and he was right, it was his house. This must have been filmed when Mags lived there.

The camera swung over to the person Mags was talking to, and Robbie thought, this can't be happening. It was Billy Strickland, and he was telling some story, but then the camera turned again and there was Tommy. The camera zoomed in and he gave it a big, loving grin, leaned forward and there was a squeal. The camera swung up to the sky and the screen went blinding white and turned into a green blur – the grass, Robbie guessed. The camera straightened out and focused on Tommy Strickland again and he was laughing, and Billy was still telling his story and Mags was still giggling, but the camera was only interested in Tommy, who was giving it a look that was partly teasing, partly possessive. There was a flash of something cold, evaluating, in his gaze.

Then Tommy was turning to his brother and listening to his story, which was about a fight outside the pub.

The camera stayed on Tommy, and after a bit he got up, looked at the lens and swaggered off towards the house. The camera followed as he went round the corner and disappeared from sight. The camera swung again, to find Mags with her arms over Billy's shoulders. The scene changed abruptly and the camera was behind Tommy, climbing the stairs, going into what was now Robbie's room, and Tommy was throwing himself on to an unmade bed saying, 'You'd better put that away.'

Robbie couldn't at first make out what was on the screen next, but the camera moved and he could see a girl's back. He heard Strickland's voice saying, 'Turn round.' She said, 'I'm not doing this for you, Tommy,' and she reached for a white dressing gown and put it on, before she turned.

It was her.

Robbie knew it would be.

'Come on,' said Tommy, wheedling.

She started to sway, running her hands through her hair.

'How do I know who you're going to show this to?'

'No one, I swear it. Do it. Do it for me, beautiful.'

'I love it when you call me that,' she said quietly.

She started to sway again, and giggled, and began to untie the dressing gown cord, then it all stopped. Robbie wondered if someone had edited it.

Suddenly the screen showed a deep red sun sinking

among clouds that looked like hair does when you've pulled a comb through it the wrong way. There was a plain down below. They were up on the beacon.

'Gorgeous,' came Mags's voice. 'My favourite place in the world, this.'

'I love coming here with you.' It was the girl, Fran, talking from behind the camera.

'Just us.'

'Just us.'

'I'm amazed you can tear yourself away from Tommy, Fran.'

'Oh, I can. It's doable.' She laughed. 'Dead trippy, this sunset.'

'When's he finishing college?'

'Next year.'

'Then he gets one of the farms, right?'

'Well, it's been hard for his mum since his dad died. She needs some help.'

'What's his mum like? I mean, I know her, but what's she really like?'

'She's okay. I mean, I think she thinks I'm too young for him.'

'Well, you are.'

'So are you.'

'Yeah, but two years not four. Or is it five? And we're just friends. Not like you two.'

'I'm seventeen. I can do what I like. Anyway, I'm not counting.'

'You stick to him like a burr.'

Don't go there, Mags, thought Robbie. Maybe I don't know much, but I know not to criticize other people's relationships.

Nothing was said for a while. There was only half the sun left. The camera tilted slightly. The world seemed filled with quiet content.

'There's something I want to show you,' said Mags. The camera turned to show her on screen, leaning against the big grey rock. 'Before the light goes.'

'Is it a secret?'

'So secret you die if you tell anyone. Maybe you'll need it one day. We all need to hide things sometimes.'

'Mags?'

'Yeah?'

'You're right. I'm crazy about him.'

'I could guess.'

'Do you think he wants the same things, Mags?'

They were walking towards the chamber, blood-red with the last rays of the sun.

There was much, much more. All of Tommy Strickland. She had filmed him everywhere, in pubs, shops, woods and fields. It was as if she was feeding off him. And he was always behaving as if he could do anything he wanted with her. Anything. It seemed ridiculous, pathetic, even, to Robbie. It began to make him feel sick.

So did the final scenes. She was following him down

a street. He kept looking round, and when he did the camera stopped, until he started walking again. He could hear Fran breathing hard, and sometimes there was a strange whimper which must have been her too, and all at once a wild screaming wail.

'*Please, Tommy.*'

He stopped and walked back towards her. There was a quiet, terrified 'oh' from Fran.

His eyes were narrowed and mean, his lips thin, his nostrils dilating. Robbie could see his fists clenching. Tommy stooped towards the camera.

'I've told you, Fran. I've told you so many times.' His voice was soft and low. 'It's over. So over I never want to see you again. Do you get me? You're a boring, little, whining little girl, you're stupid, you're ugly, I don't want you, I don't love you, I never loved you, I never even liked you. I don't care if you throw yourself in a river, or cut yourself, or any of those things you say you're going to do. I'll even lend you a razor. Do it, Fran. The world will be a better place. Now get out of my face or I swear, girl, I'll do it for you. And I mean that. And you know I could, and you know I would. And NEVER follow me again. End of the picture show.'

He lunged and the sequence stopped.

The screen turned dark green. They were in a wood. Fir trees, packed together, not much light. There was Mags, sitting on a log, smoking a cigarette. That's interesting, thought Robbie, I've never seen her do that. She was sitting in a shard of sunlight.

'I wish you wouldn't,' said Mags, looking at the camera.

'You never minded before.'

'It's not a joke any more. You're not a joke any more.'

'Was I a joke?'

'In a good way. Then in a bad way. Not now. Not at all.'

'Are you dropping me, Mags?' Her voice was flat, as if she didn't care, anyway.

'I love you. You know I love you. But you need to see a doctor. You need to get yourself sorted.'

No answer.

'Will you see a doctor? Please?'

Still no answer.

Then something different.

It was Fran. She had the camera trained on her face, which was pale and ghostly as if all the blood had been drained out of her. She was lovely, though, Strickland had been wrong about that. Her hair flooded around her face. And her eyes were deep, dark blue, sea blue. They were rolling with unhappiness. There were tears in them, but she was too far gone to cry.

'I can't live without him,' she whispered. 'I hate him for what he's done to me, but that's not enough. I can't bear the pain inside me. It won't go away. I've tried everything, but . . . nothing works long enough, it always comes back. There's only one thing I can do now.'

Something strange was happening. The screen started getting cleaner, clearer, almost as if it was real, as if it was really her looking at him, her eyes seeing, without tears somehow, into his.

'Don't run away, Robbie. Finish it.'

For a moment he couldn't move. Then, almost automatically, he replayed.

'There's only one thing I can do now.'

This time nothing changed.

'Finish it.'

So it didn't happen, he thought. It wasn't her. It wasn't her talking to him, telling him to go back. Telling him he was part of it. That he couldn't run away. She was talking about her stricken self.

Except he knew it was.

He put the memory stick in his pocket. It was time to show Mags.

He made his way out of the house, and as soon as he stepped outside there was a wild ringing in his ears. For a second he felt utterly bewildered, then he realized. The alarm. He hadn't set it properly, hadn't done whatever it was Alice had told him he had to do. But how could he remember what to do, he thought to himself bitterly, after what he had just seen?

He was running down the pavement when a police car drew alongside.

And who was in the passenger seat?

'Interesting sleepover,' said his acquaintance from the night before. Why did they always go in for sarcasm? thought Robbie. It was so undignified.

'Get in,' the policeman said crisply.

18

NOBODY SAID a thing. Not one thing.

Sheila wouldn't even look at him. Maybe he had won this time. His dad kept smiling at him and touching him awkwardly, as if he was just making sure he was real.

Sometimes, he thought to himself, everything in life is just wrong.

He was lying on his bed.

That policeman was kind of okay, really. It's strange to find people being good to you when you don't expect them to be.

'I'll come quietly,' Robbie had said to him, when he'd recovered from the shock. The shock of the police being there, plus the shock of the alarm, plus the shock of Fran.

To his surprise, he'd received a big grin in return. He'd got in the back and the policemen both turned to look at him.

'Run away from home, have you?'

'How d'you know? I mean, I could've been breaking and entering.'

'Then the alarm would've gone off when you were entering, wouldn't it? Your friend let you in?'

'Sort of.'

'We'll work something out for you. In trouble?' Robbie nodded. 'Don't worry, son. I ran away once.' There was a look on his face, as if he understood. 'Homes aren't always sweet, are they? My stepdad terrorized me and my mum. I didn't go back until he left.'

'Didn't you hate her for letting him do it?'

'Yeah, yeah, I did. For a long time.'

'He goes to see her every Sunday,' said the other one, pulling the car out into the traffic. 'He's such a softie, mate, we don't know what to do with him.'

Now he'd been back a few days, he'd been to school, and he'd said sorry to Alice, though it turned out the alarm had switched itself off after half an hour. When he told her what he'd seen, she'd been horrified.

'Poor Fran,' she said. 'Poor, poor Fran.'

'Yeah.'

'So that was who you saw in the wood?'

'Yeah.'

'That is so terrible.' She looked at him for a long time. Then she asked him what he was going to do about it, and if he had said anything to Mags. And he said no he hadn't, because he hadn't seen her.

'Well, you'd better tell her soon,' said Alice.

There was a knock at the door.

'Are you there, Robert?'

Lucy. The only person who called him that, usually when she wanted to annoy him.

'Robert?'

The handle moved.

'Robert?'

'Robbie?' That was Jess.

The door opened.

'Robbie?' said Jess again.

'Yes?'

'Lucy's just been next door, you know, Mrs Allardyce's, she's wondering whether you forgot you were supposed to go for tea on Saturday.'

'She said perhaps you could go this coming Saturday instead,' said Lucy. 'And she asked me to give you this.' She was holding an envelope.

'It's not my birthday.'

'Whatever.'

'Go on, open it,' said Jess.

Robbie didn't move.

Lucy got to her feet. 'Come on, Jessica, we're not welcome here.'

'Okay, I'll open it for you,' said Jess.

'Fine,' said Robbie, so she did.

'Just inviting you round,' she said. 'Nice picture, though.'

Robbie turned the card over. It was a picture of a white hare, running.

19

'SO YOU came,' said Mrs Allardyce. 'I'm glad.'

'Sorry about last weekend.'

'Well, we all know about that.'

'Do you?'

'Of course.'

'No one seems to have noticed at home.'

She didn't reply, but stood blinking in the sunlight, in a dress covered in flowers. There were flowers everywhere, in the pictures, on the wallpaper, and real ones on the tables. She didn't wear any make-up, and her skin seemed to Robbie grainy like porridge that's gone cold, but with a rosiness that was lovely. Rosy porridge.

The house had more light than Robbie's, and the rooms were bigger, which seemed a bit unfair, because there was only her and her husband to rattle around in it. Mr Allardyce was sitting in the kitchen reading the paper, and eyed Robbie over his glasses.

'Ah, Robbie, what an honour. An honour and a pleasure.'

'Let's go into the sitting room,' said his wife.

More light. One wall was window from floor to ceiling. The telescope, in all its glory, was at the other end of the room.

'Walking on eggshells, I should think they are,' says Mrs Allardyce. 'Tea?'

'I don't really like tea, actually, Mrs A.'

'Don't worry, we've got plenty of other things. We were just thinking we hadn't seen you in a while, we were wondering how you were getting on. It sounds terribly nosy of us, of course, but you do remind us a bit of our oldest son when he was your age. They've all gone now, all three of them, as you know, so we're, what do they call us, empty-nesters, aren't we, Hugo?' She turned to watch him pootling about in the kitchen. 'Getting some tea, I hope,' she went on. 'What will you have, Coke, lemonade?'

'Coke would be nice,' said Robbie. 'Thanks.'

'Hear that, Hugo?' she called. 'A Coca-Cola for our guest. Shall we?' She pointed to a chair. Robbie found himself facing away from the windows, one of which was open, thankfully not blinded by the sunlight but with the heat beating down on the back of his head. There was an ancient fireplace almost as tall as him, and lots of books, old and new, and the chairs were covered in dark blue and more flowers, green and red.

'I'm glad you came,' she said again.

'What's your son do now, Mrs Allardyce?' he asked.

'Mary. Call me Mary. He's a lawyer. In London.'

'Clever, then.'

'Sharp as a tack. As are you.'

'Am I?'

'Oh, yes, anyone can see that.' She laughed a little laugh as if she knew something Robbie didn't.

'Tea's up,' said Mr Allardyce, bringing a tray in.

'And how are you finding village life after the hurly-burly of the metropolis?' asked Hugo. It took Robbie a moment to work out what he meant.

''S'all right. Well, some of it's all right.'

'It's difficult for you,' said Mary, as if she was talking to no one in particular. 'Sheila's a lively woman.'

'Did you say lovely?'

'I said lively, but I'm sure she's lovely too.'

'And Alan seems happy to be back where he grew up. Green, green grass,' said Hugo.

'Making friends is always the hardest thing,' said Mary. Now she turned her gaze on Robbie as if she was expecting something.

He remembered why he was there.

'So, the picture on the card you sent me.'

'It meant something to you?' Mary asked.

'No, I've just never seen a white hare before. It made me wonder. Do they exist? I've never even heard of one.'

'They do exist quite naturally in the wild,' said Mary. He had her full attention now. 'The mountain hare changes its colour in winter, and turns snowy white.'

'Where do you find them?'

'Here and there.'

'England, Wales?'

'There are none in England or Wales.'

'Well, that's probably why I haven't seen one. And I don't know anyone who has. That's why I noticed the card.'

'I don't mean there are no white hares to be seen in England at all,' she said.

'Well, you just said there aren't any.'

'It depends on whether you have the eyes to see them. Some do. Most don't.'

'Almost nobody does,' said Hugo.

'That's right, that's right,' said Mary. 'They're very few and far between, the people who can. They're special. Very special.'

There was a hungry look in their eyes.

'So we can be sure you've never seen one yourself?' asked Hugo.

'Why, 'cos I'm not special?'

'Oh, no. You haven't been listening. We think you are.'

'Well, I've never been to Scotland or wherever.'

'In your dreams, perhaps?'

'Dreams are dreams.'

There was a little sigh from both of them.

'Do you know about dark energy?' asked Hugo, leaning forward. 'No, don't pull a face, there's a serious point to this, it's rather like, I don't know if you know this, but dogs can only see in black-and-white. Did you know that?'

'It's the sort of thing Maggie Carr might have told you. You know what she's like with her animals,' added Mary.

Mags. Was that what this was all about? Suddenly Robbie was on the alert.

'No, she never said that.'

'The point is, dogs rely on smell and hearing far more than we do. They experience the world in a very different way. Now the thing about dark energy is this. It's something that exists in the universe that we can't see, that we only learned about relatively recently. There are only a handful of things we know about the beginning of the universe. One is that it is expanding, and we know that because of the shift in the waves the galaxies are emitting, just as the sound of a siren changes in the street when it passes you. We know that the universe is full of radio waves, and that it is full of helium. Both point to a big bang, the beginning of all things, the beginning of time and matter, because both these things, the radio waves and the helium, would have been caused by the universe starting up, by the heat causing lots of high-energy radiation and the first three minutes being like a nuclear fusion reactor which made the helium.'

'Hugo,' said Mary. She'd obviously heard all this before.

'Well, the universe should be slowing down. Gravity should be making it do that. But it's not. It's accelerating. And what's more, it's denser than it should be. By about five times. So out there there's a whole lot of energy we can't see, and a whole lot of other matter we can't see. Dark energy and dark matter. And what do you think the universe would look like if we could see these things? There could be – who knows? – waves and clusters and clouds, constantly whirling and flowing and pouring over and around each other, endless differentiations of colour and form, things we cannot even imagine. Perhaps it would be like a boiling furnace, terrifying, cataclysmic, an infinite turmoil. Perhaps,' Hugo said, 'we can only see what we can bear to see.'

'Maybe dogs can see it,' Robbie said.

Hugo stared at him. Then he laughed. 'Oh, yes. Very good. Very funny.'

Mary smiled. 'It is a thought, Hugo.' She looked at Robbie. 'But you understand what he's saying don't you?'

'I think so. I can't see what's in front of my nose, sometimes.'

'Different kinds of perception,' said Hugo.

'A simple question of understanding, of using what you know. For instance, why did someone paint the word "Run" on the side of your house?'

'Someone doesn't like us.'

'Did you notice anything about the lines painted underneath it?'

'I didn't.'

'You mean someone else did?'

'No, I just mean, they were just lines, right?'

'Did Mags see them?'

'Does it matter?'

'Yes.'

'She might've.'

'And did she say anything about them? Everyone knows you two are inseparable. She must have seen them.'

'Okay.'

'So what did she say?'

'I don't know. Nothing. I can't remember.'

Mary leaned back in her chair and regarded him thoughtfully. He sensed a change of tactic coming.

'Why are you so interested in Mags, anyway?'

'What we've been saying,' began Hugo, 'applies to people too, you know.'

'Especially to people,' added Mary. Her thoughtful look became more purposeful. 'You're right about the card I sent you.'

'Am I?'

'The white hare has a very special significance. That is, it can have. Is there any more tea, Hugo?' Hugo got up and shut the window. 'It's said that a jilted lover can return in the shape of a white hare. You don't seem surprised to hear that. Perhaps you knew?

'Legends are strange things. They're not just stories, you know. Myths and legends can be truer than anything else. They tell us elemental things about ourselves, about the world we live in, about how we relate to each other. They are about the passions and fears that are inside us, that sometimes, very often, we cannot see or feel or understand ourselves. They are about the essences of our lives, which, and this is a point I want you to remember, reappear and reassert themselves time and time again. Over the decades, the centuries, the millennia.'

'So legends are real, and they happen over and over again?'

'In a way, yes. In the way I described.'

'But do you believe the story about the white hare?'

'At the moment I'm simply wondering what you believe, what you know, and what you have seen. Did you know that hares are associated with fire?' She was watching him closely. 'And you know something about fire, don't you? It's a strange thing. It's said that when a hare runs through a village, a fire will break out in one of the houses very shortly afterwards.

They don't fear fire, you know. When we burned the stubble in the old days they all stayed behind till the last, then hurled themselves through the flames. Some of them got badly singed.

'But the white hare, now the white hare is only interested in one thing, and that's her lover. She may save his life. It's been known. But in the end, she will always cause his death.'

'You could just shoot her,' Robbie said.

'Oh, it's a sin against the Holy Ghost to kill the white hare,' said Hugo.

'Not that that ever seems to make much difference in the end,' said Mary.

'So you want me to believe all this?'

'Up to you, as I said.'

'Why?'

'We have very good reasons. And we know you have seen it in your dreams. Well, no, we don't know.' She held up her hand, as if to ward off denial. 'But perhaps you have. Now I will tell you where you might fit into all this. But first I need to know – has Maggie Carr seen the white hare?'

'Yes.' Why shouldn't they know? They've told me more than I knew before, he thought to himself. It's a trade. That's all.

Mary bit her lip, as if it was the bad news she had been expecting.

'Good. Where?'

He told them about the field.

'Good boy. Mags will know the significance of what she has seen more than anyone, well, more than anyone now alive, and Maggie Carr is, always was, one of the special ones. What fools those boys were. But as for you, Robbie, well, don't forget that for all your London ways you're a local boy.'

'Me? You're kidding.'

'You're your father's son. Let me tell you something. Some years ago they found human remains at Cheddar Gorge, not far from here. They were very, very old. People were living in the gorge and around it nine thousand years ago. They took a DNA sample, and they found that a man living not ten miles away was a direct descendant of that early human being. People don't move very far, Robbie, societies don't change, and their stories, and their legends, never die, and because we can't see things doesn't mean they aren't there.'

'So what you say about the white hare and elements and emotions and all that, what's that about?'

'The brutality of love. The desperation, the tide of misery that sweeps through you when you cannot have the one you want, the pain that's left behind that you can't endure, the callousness of the heart and its tenderness and frailty. Most of us experience it at some time in our lives, and always have done.'

The way she said these things, there was something

in her voice, something from her past maybe, an understanding. Robbie shifted in his chair uneasily.

'I think my dad's kind of nervous about all this 'cos of him and my mum. I never really knew about him and Sheila, about when they got together. I think he might have seen it. Or thought he did. He might've understood those weird lines, as well.'

'Your dad. Do you think so?' There was a sudden hopeful note in Mary's voice as she asked this. Would they prefer his dad to be the one Fleet had come for? But, why would they? What have they got against him? He felt a protectiveness that took him by surprise. Leave my dad alone, he thought. He's all right, really, sort of, somewhere underneath all of me and him. And he's *my* dad. The only one I've got.

'Then there's Fran and Tommy.'

'What do you know about them?' asked Hugo. His voice sounded reedy and shrill and mean.

'Oh, just what everyone knows.'

'Fran always had problems, she was very unbalanced,' said Mary. She crossed her arms and rearranged herself. 'Fragile personality, obsessive.'

'Very unfortunate business altogether,' said Hugo. 'But all that had finished long before she, well, what she did.'

'And Mags had a thing going with the brother as well, right? Two best friends with two brothers? What happened with Mags?'

'Oh, she was never very serious about him. She just did it to keep her friend company, just for fun.'

Robbie stretched. 'I'd better get back. Thanks for the Coke and everything.'

'Welcome home, stranger,' said his dad. He was doing a crossword, and it didn't look like he had got very far. 'All very civilized, tea with the Allardyces. Not quite your scene, though, I wouldn't think.'

'This whole scene's not my scene.'

'Oddly, I'm beginning to wonder if it's your stepmother's.' He looked at Robbie over the newspaper. 'But don't get your hopes up.'

'You don't seem too bothered.'

'Oh, I suspect it's just a phase. Not sure the life suits her as much as she thought it would, that's all.'

'You okay with it, though, right?'

'I was born to it, laddie.'

'Mary Allardyce said that I'm a local boy.'

'Well, you know, roots and so on.'

'That was kind of what she was saying.'

'She comes of old stock.'

'Everyone round here does.'

'You do miss London, don't you? Can't think why.'

'You get accepted for what you are. Not for how long you've lived somewhere.'

'There are people in this village who have lived all their lives here and are still regarded with suspicion.'

'Not you, though.'

'I don't think anyone had noticed I'd left, so they were hardly surprised to see me back. Hugo Allardyce said it was like old times. We used to go fishing together, just by the bridge. Of course, he was a lot older than me. Sticklebacks, mostly. Not much you can do with them apart from put them back.'

'Have they lived here forever?'

'They go way back. Both their families. Quite a bit of old money in hers.'

'Are they related to everyone too, then?'

'Hugo's lot come from a bit further afield, but hers have farmed here for donkey's.' He put his paper down. 'Not much luck with that, I'm afraid.'

'So where does Mary Allardyce fit in?'

'Mary? Oh, well, remember the woman with the tombola at that fair? Eliza Strickland? She's her sister.'

20

'I THINK she knows what you've done,' said Alice, drumming her heels against the underside of a bench in the playground.

'Have you got a problem with it?'

'It's not for me to judge.'

'You've got a problem.'

'Well, you know, it's Mags, right?'

'I didn't know she'd find out. Not as fast as she did.'

'Listen. The word is out, from what you say. Everyone who knows anything about anything, which does not include most people and definitely not your mum and sisters —'

'Stepmum, stepsisters.'

'Never mind that. You told certain people what they wanted to know. That Fleet is here. And that Mags knows. Fran's best friend.'

'Yeah, because —'

'Never mind because. We know where this is going now. Your dad might've thought it was to do with him. Your Mary Allardyce was hoping so, that's for sure.'

'So what's going to happen?'

'Who knows? Who knows what, who knows when? You won't be seeing Mags for a while is my guess.'

'I miss her already.'

'You traded.'

'You think I betrayed her?'

'Traded. Betrayed. Yeah, I do. But I'm not blaming you. I know why you did it. You're just the one who has to live with it.'

It was turning into a very hot summer. Robbie's dad said it was the hottest he could remember. War was brewing between him and Sheila; they had reached the point where they didn't seem to be able to agree about anything. As a result, Lucy was, for once, being friendly, and she and he and Jess rolled their eyes at each other all day long.

'They're going to end up like Mags's parents, slobbing around in different houses,' said Jess.

'Have you seen Mags recently, Robbie?' asked Lucy. 'People say she's disappeared.'

'No.'

'Anything wrong with her? You'd know, wouldn't you? Where's she gone?'

'I don't know. She didn't tell me.'

'What, she just went away? I think it's weird, disappearing like that and not talking to anyone about it.'

'That's my speciality.' Neither of them took any notice.

'Well, why should she?'

'I said I don't know.'

'I reckon he does,' said Jess. 'Uh oh, there they go again.'

'What are they arguing about this time?' asked Lucy.

'I think,' said Jess, 'it's something to do with shopping.'

'Not the Wheatsheaf, then?'

'No, he forgot to get something she wanted from the village. So very soon,' Jess went on, 'Mum'll be asking us to go and get whatever it is he's forgotten.'

The door opened.

'Would one of you three mind?' It was his dad. 'We need some spaghetti.'

'Robbie,' said the sisters, as one.

'Would you?' asked his dad.

'Hey,' protested Robbie, but then he considered. 'What's it worth?'

'Pound?' said his dad hopefully.

'Five.'

'Three?'

'Done.'

'Unbelievable,' said Jess.

His dad looked pathetically grateful.

The store in the village was empty and cool, so he lingered a while, reading the newspaper headlines and inspecting some DVDs. Robbie could hear the man behind the counter talking, something about people starting heath fires.

'She's here, you see.'

The person he was talking to dropped her voice to reply.

'Do we know who it is?'

'Well, you never do. But it's obvious, we think.'

'She always gets what she wants, you know, whatever they do to try to stop it.'

'But they'll try.'

'Oh, they'll try.'

'Spaghetti?' Robbie's question seemed to take them both by surprise. The man pointed to a shelf.

'Well, as I was saying,' continued the woman.

The man watched Robbie over his spectacles.

'You gave us a bit of a surprise there, you know.' The woman surveyed him austerely, her *Daily Mail* clutched in her hand.

'You're Maggie Carr's friend, aren't you?'

'Yes. Yes, I am.'

'You haven't seen her, have you? People are getting a bit worried.'

'Haven't seen her in ages, sorry. Maybe she's got a job somewhere or something. She's hard to predict.'

'A law unto herself,' said the woman.

'Something like that. Anyway, thanks for this.'

He hurried out of the shop into the high street, but before he could turn for home he found himself faced by a mud-covered Land Rover full of the Strickland brothers and accompanying Alsatians. The doors opened and both men and dogs poured out on to the pavement.

'We might want to talk to you,' said Tommy, head on one side, holding back the dogs on their leashes.

'I'm not that interesting, sorry.'

There was only one thing to do, and there was only one way to go. Up the street, up the hill, and fast.

As he ran, he could sense one of them running behind him, straining to catch up, then his brother shouted something and he fell back. Too many witnesses around.

He stayed off the pavement to avoid people, running on the side of the road to dodge oncoming cars, and then there were brown flashes either side of him, and something hit his back. It was the dogs, not moving fast enough to bring him down, but he was aware of a blur of movement around him, he could hear their panting and feel their hot breath and he knew they were going to move in on him as soon as he slowed or slipped.

He wasn't going to be taken. He was going to take them.

He didn't know where all this energy was coming from, he'd never run like this or felt like this. It was as if he was flying, as if the road was dissolving, melting away. He was leaving the dogs behind; he could hear them barking insanely, furious they had lost him.

About two kilometres outside the village the road cut between two cliffs into deep shade, and there he slowed. His energy had evaporated and he couldn't take another step. His insides had been sucked out and he was all shrivelled skin and bone, like a scarecrow. There was a pain in his chest. He missed the running, now that he was spent, because for a while there he had been someone else. And it had felt so good, the air flowing past him and the endless movement, like being a rapidly flowing river, or an arrow unleashed.

He sank to the ground, head against his knees, arms balanced on top of them. He thought he might be blacking out. There was nothing moving in his head. There was just a humming, perhaps it was in his blood, echoes of his heart pounding. A humming, a thrumming, a memory of the earth far away, his hearing good enough to catch it, warning him to get out, but he was too drained. His body wouldn't do the smallest thing he wanted it to.

The thrumming got louder. The tone changed, to an engine whine, an engine being gunned through its gears, and down the hill came the Land Rover, the sun blazing off its windscreen.

21

THE CAR skidded to a stop with a short sizzling scrunch. Robbie could hear the dogs falling over each other inside, thumping against the seats in front. Then the car windows slid shut and muffled the barking. All was quiet, but that wasn't going to last. He felt completely exposed. He wondered if there was anyone out there, in the fields or on the roads around. He needed another car to come along. Someone to see what was about to happen. Squinting up the sides of the cliffs on either side, he saw they were overhanging hard rock, not soft sandstone good for climbing. Even if he had the energy. And he had none now.

He knew he couldn't outrun the dogs again.

He shivered. Surprising how cool it was in the shade.

The Land Rover started to back up slowly, until it stopped in front of him. They were just looking down,

Stricklands and dogs, peering at him, waiting to see what he was going to do.

The passenger window opened. It was Billy, holding a packet of fags.

'Want one?'

He nodded.

A cigarette was picked from the packet and held out to him. The dogs' tongues had covered the back window in spittle.

'Catch.' Robbie put out his hand, but the cigarette rolled off and fell on to the tarmac. Billy looked at him and pulled a sad face. 'Oops. Pick it up,' Robbie heard him say, as if he was talking to a baby.

There was a hum in the distance.

A car, a black four-wheel-drive, came down the hill, and slowed. But the Land Rover's door opened and shut and Billy's hand was on his shoulder and he was kneeling next to him lighting the cigarette and pushing it into Robbie's hand. The driver's door opened and slammed too. There was a lot of waving and halloing from the brothers. Trying to make everything look normal.

Tommy was on the other side of the Land Rover. His brother was next to Robbie. The dogs were still inside.

One last chance.

It was all in the back neck muscles. Like heading a football.

Robbie brought the point of his forehead down sharply on to the bridge of Billy's nose. Robbie had never had that much practice, but he knew the pain would swamp his victim's head. He watched him stagger backwards. It was time to go.

If he could get up the road and into the fields he could lose them in the woods. He was going back the way he came, so he knew these cliffs ended somewhere. Doors were opening and slamming shut behind him again. They would need to turn, not so easy in that gully.

He was out in the open now. Two empty fields of grass, then one of corn, then the woods. He wasn't moving as fast as he had been and he didn't know how long he'd last. He was looking for a way into the next field, he didn't want to be rushing ditches and barbed wire, but he daren't slow down either. There was a gate over to the left, and he was aiming for that, when suddenly the dogs were behind him. He could hear them, a couple of hundred metres away, and they were shortening the distance.

He was over the gate like a high-jumper, then over the next field, his vision blurring from sweat and the pain in his chest coming back fast. Up on the hill ahead where the wood ended there was a house, he could sense it better than see it.

Another stile.

He looked back.

Tommy Strickland. Far away. Cradling something in his arms.

The top of the post next to Robbie's hand blew apart, wood splintering everywhere. Then there came the sound of the shot.

Was he trying to kill him or warn him?

Robbie's head was swimming now.

He looked up at the house again. It seemed a long way away.

One last go.

One last.

Go.

Every bit of him was screaming, every bone a heavy weight.

Stop thinking, Robbie. Stop thinking. Too much energy, thinking. Just run.

House. Where?

Come on.

Dogs. Where?

Closing. Everything closing. Me on the house. Dogs on me.

Gun. Where?

No more shots.

Warning, then.

Why would he kill me, anyway?

Whole body saying stop. Shutting down.

Almost there. Look up. Look up.

High fences. Barbed wire.

I can't get in.

Then the dogs were upon him, their teeth pulling at his clothes. As he stumbled his hand felt wood, a branch blown to the ground in the wind, long and bendy and leafy. He picked it up and brought it down on the head of one of the dogs.

The dog backed off. It wasn't expecting that.

There was strength in his arms even if his legs had gone, but as a weapon the branch was pretty lame.

They were waiting for their chance, the three of them, teeth bared, one stock-still with taut haunches, the other two sloping around him. He wasn't going to last long, he could feel that. He could see the Stricklands closing in up the hill and heaving the branch around, pushing it at the dogs, was doing him no good. No good at all.

One last burn.

Now.

He turned again and ran.

They'd been waiting for just that moment.

There was snarling in his ears, and in a blur he was down, floundering under the attack.

And suddenly there they were. Billy had blood all over his face. That wasn't a good idea, that, Robbie thought.

With his good eye, he winked at Robbie.

'Time for some fun,' he said.

22

ROBBIE COULDN'T move. His hands and feet were tied.

He could feel, though. He could do that. His whole body was consumed with pain, not all of it the same pain. The top of his head felt as if he had been scalped. There was dried blood on the side of his head, and one of his eyes had closed.

He thought he might lose consciousness. There were a lot of flies around, it must have been the blood. He could see it on his t-shirt. He rolled over and was sick over the side of the sofa he was lying on, which smelled of cat's piss.

He had taken everything he could now. He couldn't be hurt any more.

He was in a big barn with a high roof, filled with junk. There was lots of rusty machinery, and the tractor and the Land Rover he could remember from his previous visit. As the flickering in his head slowed and the pain receded he could see the light outside was fading. The great doors were silhouetted in the dusk, and against the wall there were bales of sweet-smelling straw.

He wondered how long he'd been there.

He had a thirst that made his throat feel like sandpaper.

He wondered if anyone was out looking for him.

You know, Robbie, he thought to himself, this might not have a happy ending. And he didn't even know what they wanted.

Actually, that wasn't true. He knew exactly what they wanted, what he had over them. They wanted what they thought he knew.

He only had that one card, but it was a trump. He had to play it well.

He was beginning to drift again. He tried to roll over to get his head away from the cat smell, and then he got the smell of his own sick. The rope, or whatever it was around his wrists, was tight and his hands were sore from lying on them. He wondered if this was the first time the Stricklands had done this.

A light went on.

'Oh, he's been sick.'

They were behind him.

'The little lamb. Dear, dear me.'

Now they were looking down at him, and Tommy was turning something over in his right hand, long and thin and shiny, which Robbie didn't like one bit.

The younger brother reached out and pulled him upright, kicking his feet so they swung into line. They got some old chairs from the back of the barn and slammed them down in front of him, sitting on them and folding their arms. The knife blade flashed in Tommy's hand as the reflected light shone momentarily into Robbie's eyes.

Flash, flash.

'You like running away, don't you?' said Tommy. 'Nobody's going to be surprised much.'

'Maybe you could tell me what this is about? It seems kind of excessive.'

'You ran away from us.'

'Like you said, I like running.'

'Why did you do that?'

'I'm guessing I'm not top of your friends list, right?'

'Maybe. But there's only a little something we need to know, and we're thinking you could help.'

'And that is?'

'Where's Maggie Carr?' said Billy.

'I don't know.'

'Man, we hit you enough, you want some more?' said Tommy.

'I don't know where Mags is.'

'You don't know? Yeah, you know,' said Billy, leaning forward in his chair.

Don't start again, mate, please don't, thought Robbie. This head's falling apart already.

'Why would I? She didn't tell me she was going anywhere.'

'When did you last see her?'

'I don't know. Before she left, I s'pose.'

Billy looked as if he was going to make a move, but Tommy waved a hand to stop him.

Flash, flash.

'It was at her dad's house.'

'What were you doing there?'

'Just watching TV and stuff.'

'What were you watching?'

'Can't remember.'

'Mags's dad doesn't have a TV.'

'Yes, he does.'

'Not one that works.'

'Well, I was watching it.'

'No, you weren't. Want to know why? He owes us money, right? But he doesn't pay it. So Billy goes to see him and, weirdly, somehow his foot goes straight through the TV screen. Imagine that.'

'Yeah, weird,' said Billy.

'An accident,' said Tommy.

'Easy to do,' Robbie said. 'Anyway, he must've got a new one.'

'Thing is,' said Billy.

'Every time he gets a new one, Billy goes over and there's this accident again.'

'So weird,' said Billy.

'So I think you probably weren't watching TV with Mags,' said Tommy. He got up and walked behind Robbie.

Suddenly Tommy was pulling up his arms and pain was shooting along them.

For a moment he thought it was all over and tensed, waiting for the first thrust of the blade. But instead he found his arms swinging back round in front of him and he could move them. He'd been cut free. Billy looked at his brother as if he thought he'd gone mad, but Tommy just jerked his head and Billy slunk sullenly off into the darkness.

Tommy sat down again with his feet up on his brother's chair. He brushed his hair casually back over his head and stared up into the recesses of the barn roof.

'Feet?' Robbie asked hopefully.

'Feet can wait,' Tommy said. 'See, Robbie,' he went on, 'it's really important I find Mags.'

'Yeah, I know.'

'You know why?'

'No.'

'You sound like maybe you do.'

'No, I was just, I mean, I could get that, like, from what you were saying.'

'And, until you tell me where she is, you're staying here.'

'And then what?'

'So you do know something? You must know something or you wouldn't be thinking you'll be getting out of here.'

'My head hurts, I'm not getting this.'

'Yeah, I'm sorry about that.'

'*You're* sorry?'

'It's a bad idea to upset Billy. Lots of people find that out. The best thing is to keep him smiling.'

'I'll try to remember.'

'We heard there was something you told someone about something she'd seen.'

'You want to be more specific?'

'You know what I'm saying.'

'So this is my fault, right?'

'No. 'Cos now I know. I know what she's seen. What I need to find out is what she's doing about it.'

'Well, I don't know. Last time I saw her, I mean the real last time, was just down on that bridge, where we always hang out.'

'Cute.'

'She's not my girlfriend.'

''Course she isn't, you little runt.'

'So that's all I know. I mean, I s'pose she doesn't trust me now, so she's not going to tell me anything, is she?'

This went home. Tommy got up and walked about, his boots thumping on the concrete floor.

'So what's happening to me?'

'You're staying here. Like I said.'

'You going to feed me? I really need something to drink.'

Robbie started unwinding the rope around his ankles. Tommy didn't try to stop him, but stood in front of him, looking at him long and hard. Robbie thought, they're going to try and work me over again some time, and I so don't want to be around for that.

But all Tommy said was, 'She's out there somewhere.'

And Robbie knew it wasn't Mags he was talking about. Something in Tommy's voice nearly made Robbie feel sorry for him.

'I'll give you the night to think about it,' Tommy said. Then he was gone. Robbie heard the key turn in the lock.

The barn doors looked solid, and apart from them there was the one back door with a cat flap in it. Up in the ceiling there were skylights, but there were no ladders around to help him reach them. There was some water in a bowl for the farm cats, it looked disgusting, but he didn't have a choice. He took a sip, spat it out, then forced himself to drink some more.

Okay, what else did he have on him? No phone, they'd taken that, it was locked so they couldn't use it.

He still had his lighter, but no cigarettes. And that was about it.

The barn was rank. Broken boxes, a dilapidated boat and three sets of oars, two rusting engines, some empty plastic containers that smelled like they'd had cider in them, a length of green hose hanging on the wall. Four tables, one that had been used for table tennis. White goods – clapped-out fridges and washing machines. There was something that looked as if it had once been an iron staircase lying on its side. Some bookcases. The old tractor and the Land Rover.

The tractor had lost its engine; maybe it was one of the two lying by the wall like big broken hearts. It was sitting at the top of a shallow ramp that sloped to the doors.

The thing about the Land Rover was, did it have a lock on its fuel tank? To Robbie's surprise and relief, it didn't. This might all just turn out to be possible.

So this was his plan. Get the hose, cut it on the edge of the iron staircase, put it in the tank, suck hard and siphon the petrol into the plastic container.

All he needed was some light to see what he was going to be running into out there. He wasn't going to sleep, that was for sure. He needed to sit tight and wait, and he was going to have to be very, very speedy.

Finally, dawn came. There was light in the sky and through the gap between the barn door and the concrete floor Robbie could spy the outline of the farm buildings. There was the barn with one side open to the world over to the right that he remembered from before, and another beyond it, and behind that the ground rose to a ridge.

He was on the old tractor beginning to ease off the brake.

It happened so fast it was over in a second. He was lying nearly out cold by the tractor and the door had been broken open, only a bit, but enough, held there by the tractor's nose. His head was spinning again. He hadn't thought it would work at all really, so he hadn't considered the effect of the impact.

He squirmed through the gap in the door with the container full of petrol, heading for the next barn, taking off the cap from the container and swinging it so the petrol sprayed all over the back of the barn wall.

A door slammed. He waited.

There was a shout from Billy, 'Robbie?' He must have made a bit of a racket. 'You won't get far. You know what Tommy can do with a gun.'

Robbie took out his lighter.

The flames blew up the side of the barn with that sweet soft sound and then they took hold. It was a bone-dry summer. Perfect.

He ran up the hill, and by the time he looked back the flames were piling into the sky. It was beautiful in the early dawn light, like big sails billowing on before a yacht.

He could see Tommy running towards the barn, carrying two buckets of water. He was going into the barn. What was he doing that for? It could collapse any second. The fire's way too big for him. That barn's going to go, and he's going to be inside it.

There was a wild feeling rising in Robbie: it was panic and it was fear, and in a weird, weird way he wanted to protect Tommy, who was hurrying back again with more buckets. Where was Billy? They'd be calling the fire brigade, he'd better go. But he couldn't move. Tommy was going inside the barn again.

There was something else in the yard. At first Robbie thought it was Billy, wearing a white hat, or a white hoodie or jacket or something. But it wasn't. It was white, though.

It was her.

Just sitting there.

There was a yelling like a thousand devils. Billy was running out of the house, calling Tommy, pointing at Fleet, raising his gun.

She didn't move, she stayed still. The light from the dawn seemed to flow into her, she was luminous, like the first time he'd seen her.

Time slowed.

Nothing happened. Nothing moved.

Then Tommy came running out of the barn.

With a roar the roof crashed down.

At the same time Fleet ran and there was a shot.

It was as if Robbie's insides flooded with acid, with flames.

But Billy had missed. She was away so fast Robbie could hardly see where she went. The speed of light. Of moonlight, of dawn light.

She had saved her lover.

Just as Mary Allardyce had said she might.

23

THERE WAS no one around at home. Robbie let himself in and headed up to his room, needing sleep.

When he woke it was late morning, and still there was no one around, so he fixed himself some cereal. The house was deserted and a little bit messy, which was not Sheila's style at all. As he ate, he heard a scraping sound from the garden, and went out. His dad was working the soil over with a hoe. He didn't look in the mood for company.

'Dad?'

His dad sighed and, without looking round, stopped what he was doing and leaned his chin on the hoe, gazing listlessly into the distance.

'Where is everybody?' Robbie asked.

'They've gone,' his dad replied.

'What d'you mean, gone?'

'They've gone to London.' His dad turned back to

his flowerbed. Scrape, scrape went the hoe. 'I don't think they'll be returning.'

'Why not?'

'Sheila and I had a bit of an argument last night.'

'That bad?'

'That bad.'

'What was it about?'

'I don't particularly want to rehearse it now. It might have helped if you had come back with some spaghetti.'

The spaghetti. It must be lying in the road somewhere.

'You argued over spaghetti?'

'More about the fact that you didn't bring it back. Sheila made some rather pointed remarks.'

'She slagged me off?'

His dad pursed his lips. 'She was pretty scathing. And though a large part of me agrees with her . . . where did you go, anyway? And did you come back at all? I didn't hear you come in.'

'I had a bit of a run-in with the Stricklands. But, yeah, I came back all right. I kept quiet, though.' And you can blame me however much you like, Dad, he thought, but I'm not taking it.

'I'm not surprised if you heard us arguing.'

'Well, I didn't know what it was about, and I was tired, so I went to bed.'

'Very sensible. What happened with the Strickland

boys?' He came out of his reverie and, looking at his son for the first time, recoiled in alarm. Instinctively, he put his hand on Robbie's arm. Robbie flinched in irritation. 'Jesus Christ, what happened to you? Did they do this? You look as if you've been in a war zone. Listen, let's get some ice on that eye and get you to a doctor.' He stroked his son's cheek, and Robbie flinched again, this time from pain. 'Come on, we're getting the police in too. I'm not having this. Bloody hell.' He was becoming agitated.

'Dad, it was nothing I couldn't handle. Bad fall, that's all. Leave the police out of it. I mean it. Really. I lost the spaghetti, though. So were you defending me?'

'Well, I wouldn't want you to think the whole thing was about you.'

'That's a relief.'

'It hasn't been an entirely successful enterprise for some time.'

'You're talking about Sheila, right?'

'Yes, of course. What else would I be talking about?'

'Well, call it a relationship, then. Unless you don't want to get back together. You don't want to, do you?'

'What?'

'Get back together.'

His dad pushed out his lower lip, squidged up his nose and pulled his mouth down at the corners. Looks like it's going to be just me and him for a while, thought Robbie.

'We'll have to see how it all pans out. Come on, let's see what we can do for that face of yours.'

'I'll miss her cooking.'

'You were never really that sold on her, Robbie, I know.'

'I did like Jess, though.'

A little later, he texted her: '???'

She texted back: '!!!'

He replied, 'Any chance of a rematch?'

She came back with, 'Negative c u when we grown up.'

Which did seem a bit final.

24

AUGUST. THE FIELDS were beginning to be full of harvesters pouring grain into trucks, and the roads were full of harvesters and trucks getting in everyone's way.

Robbie suspected that his dad thought that deep down Robbie was disturbed by him and Sheila splitting up, and Robbie wanted to say to him, 'Dad, I was disturbed by you and Sheila getting together.'

Surprisingly, given what he'd done, the Stricklands seemed to have lost interest in him. Alice thought they would be terrified now.

'They'll be looking, but not for you,' she said. 'Everyone will be. Everyone who knows, who's in with that family.'

'Most people try and keep out of their way.'

'My guess is they've got lots of friends and their enemies are scared of them and there's going to be a core who know all about this stuff. All of it. I said that to you.'

'I could go snooping round the Allardyces' house.'

'You won't get anything from them.'

'So we just sit and wait.'

'I was going to say it's not our problem, but, Robbie, you're in this somehow, and that's for a reason. It's you, it's your dad, it's your mum, it's something.'

'Mags.'

'Yeah, Mags.'

'I was in it from the start with her.'

'Yes,' she said. 'Yes.'

More and more he thought about Mags. *Finish it*, Fran had said. But he couldn't without Mags. And he wasn't even sure Fran was talking to him, maybe she was just talking to whoever was watching, whoever found the memory stick. Maybe she thought Mags would find it, she was the obvious one. But there was anxiousness everywhere now, in the air, in the heat and the dust, and in the endless noise from the roads and fields.

He remembered Mags saying, 'I'm worried about you and your dad.'

'Why?' he had asked.

'You need him. He needs you. And you just ignore him.'

'He's a loser.'

'You always say that, and no, he's not. He works hard. He does his best for you.'

'This is my dad you're talking about?'

'Don't be like that. He's all you've got.'

'I've got no one. I'm on my own. Apart from you, Mags. And Alice.'

She seemed not to be listening, just looking at him with those pale eyes, a little kink in her forehead.

'You need him, Robbie. And he loves you.'

'How do you know?'

'I can tell.'

'How?'

'The way he looks at you. The way he talks about you.'

'I've never heard him talk like he loves me.'

'Not when you're there, you wazzock. That's the way he is.'

'Am I like that?'

'Sometimes. Often. Not when you're thinking about your mum, though. And you're still angry.'

'Not these days.'

'Maybe. But there's so much going on in there that doesn't come out.' She pointed a forefinger at his heart.

Being Mags, of course she was right, but he was right too. He didn't think he was as crazy as he had been, in fact, he knew he wasn't, and she'd had a lot to do with that. He wasn't so impulsive, so ambushed by life. He no longer felt he was running away from everything, and, if this didn't sound a little bit cheesy, maybe he was finding a way of running towards something, though he wasn't sure what it was yet. Maybe they would sell the house and go back to London. But then he wouldn't see Mags. And for the first time, he thought, he didn't need London as much as he thought he had after all. He was beginning to feel part of the slow rhythm of the seasons, the opening up of spring, the serenity of summer. He knew the names of the trees now, and all sorts of other things, such as the likely movement of the cattle and who the flocks belonged to. He and his dad had this in common, at least. The land was claiming him. There was a life to be had here.

Then there was Fran. Poor besotted Fran. She was the clue to everything, why everything was happening the way it was, why people were doing and saying what they were. She was at the centre of it all, she was like the blood pulsing through the world, a drum beating, on to the end. Robbie remembered Mrs Allardyce's words. *The brutality of love, the pain that's left behind.* For all Mags says, you've got to be careful with your heart.

He thought of that glade in the woods with the faded flowers tied to the tree.

Outside his house at the back were his dad's favourite late summer dahlias, and he went to cut some, bright blood-red, their petals swirling geometrically.

On the other side of the fence Hugo Allardyce walked past the corner of his house. He was wearing shorts and trainers and carrying a walking stick. He looked in Robbie's direction, then turned away as if he'd never seen him before.

Robbie found some rubber bands in his dad's desk to put round the dahlia stems, and got some tape from the shed in the garden to bind them to the tree.

When he reached the wood it was very still and out of the sun the sweat on his back began to cool. He hadn't visited the place since he'd first seen her, and it felt as if it had lost its innocence, or, worse, somehow become contaminated.

The cooling sweat turned to the chill of something else. There was no one around, and he was walking towards a place of death. A place where pain, too much pain, had been extinguished. And the trees had gone on growing, and the sun beat down on the leaves above.

A girl was sitting on the little bank where the dip began. Most of the dried leaves had gone, broken up and dissolved into the bare earth under the trees.

He stopped and stared. She was blonde, her knees were under her chin, and she was looking at the tree where the flowers had been tied. She was wearing a denim jacket. The flowers were new.

It was her. *The friendless one.*

Alone.

His heart began to pound. His senses were open wide. He could feel every sound from far away, cars and trucks on the roads and sheep up on the beacon, every soft scent of the brackeny wood, every stroke of the sun.

Once more the stillness was alive.

For a long time he waited, watching her. She didn't move, and he couldn't see her face.

What would happen this time?

She turned.

He was wrong.

'You going to say hello?' she said, just like when they'd first met.

He was so relieved he could have cried.

'Mags.'

She stood up and threw her arms around him.

'I thought you hated me.'

'I did.'

'So what changed? Where've you been?'

'Hiding. You know me. And I heard about what those guys did to you, and what you did to them, and everything else, and I was worried about you, and I was proud of you. And then I knew it was time.'

'Time for what?'

'Time for some things to happen. I can feel it. You can feel it.' Her eyes narrowed as she looked at him. 'But that was a mean thing you did. A bad thing. It got me into a pile of trouble.'

'I'm sorry.'

'Why did you do that? Why did you tell them?'

'I didn't mean to. I don't think I knew what I was doing. And I didn't know who she was.'

'Eliza Strickland's sister. Just the worst person you could have told about me and Fleet. Apart from Eliza, of course.'

There was a silence between them. He placed his flowers on the tree beside hers.

Mags looked at him and shook her head, but there was no real venom there, he could tell. He felt stupid, and sorry, and just not sure, as he hadn't been all the time since, whether he'd done something wrong there because he meant to, because he was being too inquisitive, because he was happy to betray what Mags knew, or all those things. Sometimes it's hard to know how guilty you are.

She smiled her graceful, pearly smile.

'Here's an idea. You want to go swimming?'

He knew there was a pool nearby, his dad had mentioned it a few times, but he'd never looked for it. He'd always supposed it would be crowded, but when they got there it was deserted, despite the heat. And it was beautiful; a river ran into it and out the other side and it was deep and clear between low mossy cliffs with big slabs of rock on its floor. Robbie sat on the edge and watched Mags strip and for a moment she seemed different to him. She dived in perfectly with hardly a ripple. He watched her slipping through the water, scaring the trout lying lazily at the bottom and he knew he had to try it. When he was in Mags started chasing him and for a while there was nothing but shrieking and splashing and the sun catching in the spray and the pool swirling around them.

They lay in the sun to dry off, then they pulled on their clothes and Robbie found himself getting sleepy. Mags kept kicking him with her foot because she was getting bored, and eventually she got up and said she was off for a walk. Robbie moved his head into the shade, listening to the murmur of the river. Sleep began to paw at him, and his eyes got heavy.

He hardly knew where he was when he woke up. He wasn't sure how long he'd been asleep, and for a fraction of a moment he couldn't even remember why he was there.

He remembered Mags was walking somewhere in the woods, and he went on listening to the sound of running water, thinking about them swimming, the light under the surface, the shock of the cold clenching water and the warm sun opening them up.

He saw Mags at the top of the bank, staring down, her face in dark shadow. He waved to her and smiled. But she didn't respond. She was watching something in the water.

He looked down, expecting to see her reflection, but instead he saw something white.

A white hare, her ears like two flames.

The cat of the wood.

He looked up at the bank. Nothing.

He looked back into the water. Nothing.

The hare and the girl had gone.

'Robbie.'

He let out a shout and spun to face her.

'Are you okay?' It was Mags, coming quietly out of the woods without warning.

She looked into his eyes. 'What have you seen?' she asked.

'I thought I saw you.'

'She's been here, then,' she said to herself. 'Sorry.' She stroked his face. 'I shouldn't've left you. Try to concentrate. You've had a shock. What did you see?'

'I thought it was you,' he said again. His heart was pounding. 'Up on the bank. But she wasn't looking at me, she was looking in the water. And her reflection wasn't her. It was a white hare. Her. Fleet.'

'Yes. Of course.'

'Mags, am I going mad?'

'No, no. It could drive you mad, though. That's why I've said so little. I was trying to tell you that up on the beacon, after you ran away. But we're too far in now. Too far in.' She drew a deep breath. 'Think reflections. If you see the hare in a mirror you'll see the person she really is, or who she really was. It's all in the stories. And it works in reverse. If the woman is reflected, you'll see the hare. They're in different dimensions, but they're twinned with each other. Forever. Inseparable.'

'That's sad,' Robbie said, not understanding.

'Is it?'

'So what happens now?'

'She's very near,' said Mags.

'What does that mean?'

'They've got walkers out everywhere, looking for her, looking for me.'

Mr Allardyce in his shorts, thought Robbie.

'They won't find her, though, will they?'

'Somehow, somewhere, they'll meet. The lovers. They have to. They always do.'

'We can't do anything, then,' he said.

'We need to be there.'

'Why?'

Mags said nothing.

'Mags?' he asked.

She started playing with her hair, undoing it and doing it up again.

'Mags?' he asked again.

'She was my best friend.'

'Are you going to try and help her, Mags?' he asked.

She shook her head. 'No,' she said. 'No. But she'll need me.'

'So can we work out where she's going to be?'

'Sometimes,' said Mags, 'she appears near to where she was first seen.'

'That field,' said Robbie.

'Maybe.'

'But the Stricklands and their friends won't know that,' he said, and then he remembered. 'The trouble is, actually, they do,' he said.

'You didn't,' she said.

'I did. I'd forgotten.'

She stared at him in fury.

'Sorry,' he said. 'On the other hand . . .'

'What?'

'It kind of makes it easier, right? If it's all going to happen anyway, it'll just happen faster.'

'They'll be prepared, though.' Mags was so angry her voice was tight in the back of her throat. For a while she said nothing.

Then, finally, she let it go.

'In the old days when the white hare came they'd burn the stubble,' she went on. 'That's one of the hare's names, from the poem: the stag of the stubble. They'd start on one side of the field and work to the other. When the animals in the field broke cover, the guns had them. That's how they flushed her out. But they never knew whether she was there, and often she wasn't, and instead, somewhere, somehow, later she'd be revenged. And now they'll be ready for her.'

'Mrs Allardyce said the hare rarely fails.' He went on, 'So will they burn the field?'

'It depends what it's had in it. Stubble burning's not allowed any more, it's been banned for years. Bad for the soil. There are so many pollution restrictions now, it's hard to set fire to anything. But when someone's desperate, well, in late summer fires can start very easily. They'll try anything, those boys, at the best of times, and for them, or one of them, this is the worst. They've got to find her before she finds them.'

'So they flush out the animals. Does that work?'

'The thing is, hares aren't afraid of fire. A bit like you.'

'Mrs Allardyce said. They jump through it.'

'Maybe that's the connection,' said Mags. 'Is that your affinity, Robbie? Is it fire?'

He shrugged. 'Who knows?'

'They'll jump through the fire if they think it's less of a threat than a line of men with guns,' Mags went on.

'You can't kill a ghost.'

'She's not a ghost, she's not a pretend hare, she's flesh and blood and needs to eat and drink and she's out there in the fields like the ordinary ones.'

'So she might be in that field and she might not, and the Stricklands might have a go at her and they might not, but one way or another we know something's going to happen. What do we do?'

'We watch. And we wait. It's only a matter of time.'

25

MAGS WAS entirely focused on Fleet now. She seemed to know what everyone was saying, and especially where the Stricklands were, where they were going next, everything about them. He didn't know how she did it; it was as if she even knew what the wind was thinking. And she had been right about the walkers, the roads were crawling with them. The Allardyces were never at home. Mags said that because they didn't know where Fleet would be, they would try everywhere but the field where she'd first appeared, until the last moment. It wouldn't be harvested for a while yet, anyway.

She had become almost invisible. She was so brown, and the clothes she was wearing so weathered and faded that she melted into the landscape and became part of it. She had an intense awareness of everything around her, as if she could read the future in the ink-blue silhouettes the sun cast on the leaves, or in the white tyre tracks of cloud far above. And still no one knew where she was, save Robbie. They spent their days walking the fields and woods and lanes, looking, watching, waiting.

These were the hottest days of the year, the heat making them long for the tree-shade, and they lay panting in it like dogs.

'Remember when we first saw her?' Robbie said, one afternoon, under trees not far from the beacon, looking out over the Levels. 'She was so big. And there was so much light.'

'Yeah,' said Mags. He could tell she wasn't listening.

'Mags?'

'Yeah?'

'What was she like?'

'Fran?' She stopped to think for a while. 'She was so fun. On for anything. Had a wild streak, that girl.'

'Like you.'

'Different wild. And she could be up, but she had this quiet side, like she'd get really thoughtful and not talk to you. Maybe that was a bad side.'

'Manic,' he replied.

'What's that?'

'Kind of up and down. Never in-between.'

'Well, that's the way she was.'

'I like her.'

'Yeah, you should. She'd like you.' Mags was lying on her front, weaving grass. Then she looked at him curiously, as if he'd said something she couldn't quite hear. 'I've been stupid,' she said.

'What, about Fran?'

'No, no.' She pulled herself up on to her knees. 'It's what you said. Light. There was lots of light. It was a full moon.'

'It was huge.'

'No, it was full. The full moon. No, wait. The harvest moon. That's it. The harvest moon. The harvest. D'you get it?'

'Not really.'

'The harvest. The time for reaping what has been sown.'

'What is a harvest moon?'

'It's in September. All full moons rise around sunset, but the harvest moon rises faster, so there's more light around earlier in the evening, and the farmers used to be able to bring in their crops by it.'

'So what are you thinking?'

'Not thinking, feeling. Just feeling.'

'The next full moon, then?'

'Could be. We'll watch the field. It's only a few days away.'

'Which do you think she'd go for? This one or the harvest?'

'I think I know which she'll go for. I think I do. The harvest. But we'll still watch the field.'

~

So they went back to where it had all begun. But now there was corn growing tall, and they couldn't see over it or through it.

'This is insane,' said Robbie after they'd been there a couple of hours.

The sun had gone down, and the moon was rising. It was very still. Mags and he were making their way like two little spiders around the edge of the field.

Something cracked loudly, in among the trees.

Robbie hugged the ground.

Everything stayed calm. Mags raised herself cautiously.

'What can you see?' he breathed.

'It's them.'

They lay quiet for a while.

'They still there?'

'I think they've gone.'

'They're not idiots, then.'

'Yeah, you're probably right. I don't think it's tonight, and neither do they. They think it's the moon, though, too.'

'Mags?'

'Yeah?'

'You know I've got school starting soon?'

'And your point is?'

'I won't be around so much.'

'That's okay.'

'But you'll be on your own.'

'So?'

'You need someone to look after you.'

There was a quiet explosion of laughter.

'You think you're looking after me?'

'Someone's got to.'

'Believe me, I don't need you to do that.'

'Yes, you do.'

'Robbie, I know this place like I made it myself. I know every stone and tree, where the cows go when it's noon in July, which trees were felled that shouldn't have been and what they did with them, who hates who, who loves who that shouldn't – d'you see? This is my world. I'm as safe here as I'll ever be anywhere.'

Term started again. Mags seemed despondent, and it wasn't because of Robbie.

'It's gone quiet,' she said. 'The walkers have disappeared. As if they've forgotten all about it. Maybe they think she's gone away.'

'Does she ever?'

'No, never.'

'They'll know that. They'll know she's coming.'

Mags didn't seem impressed, and he didn't see much of her for days. Sometimes he glimpsed her far away, on top of a hill, tiny against the sky, walking sullenly along, sometimes he caught up with her down by the river, distracted, dreamy and a bit snappy, half in this world, half in a world where he couldn't follow.

And so they went on waiting, while the moon fattened.

26

WHEN THE day came it was a beauty. Warm as toast, a bright blue sky, everything bathed in golden September light. Mags was waiting for him, and they walked down to the bus stop together.

'Are you going to watch that field all day?'

'Yeah.'

'How will they know when to burn it?'

'I don't know. None of this makes sense, not the sense you want it to make.'

There was tiredness in her voice, as if she was stretched and emptied at the same time. Maybe she was just exhausted, but Robbie thought there was more to it.

'Still quiet?'

'Oh, no,' she said, which he hadn't expected. 'They're out again. There've been sightings, just the last two days.'

'So it's happening, this time?'

'I suppose it must be.'

'You okay, Mags?'

'I think so. Not sure.' She looked at him with her big blue eyes in her little pale face. 'I feel so weak, I don't know why.'

'She needs you to help her now.'

'I can't help her like this.'

'I don't mean like that. I think she's using your strength.'

'Maybe. I don't know. Why should that be? And why me? I suppose that's obvious.' She looked at him as if she was searching for something, but she might just have been looking through him, thinking it all over. Then she said, 'We'll have to follow her.'

'Sorry?'

'We'll have to follow her. Afterwards. If there is an afterwards. If she escapes, she'll run.'

'We can't keep pace with a running hare.'

'You can. I think you can.'

'Dogs, maybe. Not a hare.'

'Someone has to.'

'Why?'

'I don't know.' The tension was back in her voice. She sounded as if she was about to snap. Robbie put his arms round her and she folded into them.

~

When he came home from school he'd been texting Mags all day. She had seen no one, nothing. He gave his dad the slip, and when he found her, lying by the side of the field in the same place they'd been before, she was asleep. She looked so peaceful it seemed a shame to wake her, and when he did she started, as if from shock, and looked at him blankly for a moment.

'Oh,' she said. 'Robbie. It's you.'

He looked out over the field. Since the last full moon the corn had been cut and it was covered in stubble. The sun was sinking steadily.

Somewhere out there . . .

'So – nothing?'

'No. But that's interesting.' She pointed to a pile of hay in the far corner of the field.

'Why?'

'People don't leave stuff lying around like that. Not unless it's for something special.'

'You sure?'

'Kind of. I might be wrong.'

'I bet you're not.'

As the sun sank the sky was flooded with crimson and the edges of the white clouds above them shone.

'Awesome,' said Robbie to no one in particular.

Night came on. A wind sprang up.

In a gap between the trees hung the harvest moon.

'Something's stirring. Look,' said Mags.

A light leaped up on the other side of the field.

A man was holding a flame and another was standing watching.

'It's them,' said Mags. 'That's Tommy with the burning rag, I think that's what it is, on the end of a stick. Must be soaked in petrol.'

Tommy plunged the stick into the little hayrick and they both watched as it caught fire. The rick began to burn, and the moon climbed higher.

'It's hard to see.'

'It'll get better.'

As the rick blazed the men took forkfuls of it and began laying them in the stubble, and the breeze swept the flames forward so they took hold. Soon almost half of the field was on fire, spreading slowly towards the other side. Robbie's heart beat hard with the fierceness of it. The air was full of drifting clouds of bitter smoke. Animals started to run – rabbits, hares, those were the ones he could see, there must have been hundreds of others, mice and rats and snakes and voles. The field rippled with movement. One of the Stricklands disappeared through a gate for a moment, then drove a flatbed truck down the edge of the field to face the incoming flames. There was a searchlight in the back.

Billy Strickland had his shotgun poised and ready at his shoulder.

Brightness flooded the field from the top of the truck. Tommy was working it, standing behind the cab. He had a gun too. A hare hesitated in the glare and bounded back towards the fires. Without stopping it hurled itself through the smoke and flames, looking for the patches left unburned, leaping through the smouldering wreckage of the field.

The beam swept the field.

'Let's go,' whispered Mags. They slid on their fronts along the ditch. It was made easy for them by the noise of the fire, but it took time to crawl half a field's length, and when they surfaced they'd come further than they thought, ten or twenty metres behind the Stricklands.

Billy was striding up and down, his gun now low and horizontal, as if he meant to shoot from the hip. The searchlight was swaying from side to side.

'She's not coming,' said Robbie.

'She's here,' said Mags.

He looked at her sharply. Her voice sounded slurred, as if she could hardly drag the words out, and she was white, dead white, under the blaze of the moon. She was struggling to keep her eyes open.

'I can't see her.'

Mags didn't say anything.

Then the searchlight stopped.

And there she was.

Robbie didn't know if it was a trick of the light or whatever, the way eyes can be in bright light, in camera flashes, for instance, but Fleet's eyes were shining red. And she was sitting there bristling with fury, her ears tall and terrible.

The brothers started shooting. The noise was deafening. For a moment Fleet stayed where she was, then started to lope backwards and forwards across the searchlight beam.

Don't. Don't do that, Robbie thought.

Run.

Do something.

Run.

There was a shout from Tommy. Fleet had been spun round by his shot, and as she turned to face the light a wound on her back leg glistened with blood. She limped sideways, and the beam followed, but couldn't find her. This time the shout was angry, and there was fear in it too.

Because she had disappeared.

The searchlight swung madly.

Suddenly she was there again, running in from some-where, under Billy, between his legs. And he was falling, so fast Robbie could only see it when he thought about it afterwards, twisting, throwing out his left hand, his right holding the gun whirling fast, out of control, towards Tommy.

One barrel of shot was all it needed, spraying wide.

Then it was quiet. Long, lingering quiet that settled in as the crackle of the burning stubble subsided.

Until a sound bubbled up, and after a while Robbie realized what it was.

It was Billy, sobbing.

27

MAGS WASN'T moving, her head was on the ground as if she'd given up at last. She'd gone too, far away.

What had she said? Follow her? How can you follow something you can't see in a field in moonlight? But the moonlight was very bright now. It was pure, very white.

The flames were inching towards Billy. They had reached the truck. The tyres started to go one after another, the truck jumping as they blew. Billy stomped through the fire, gunning the engine into reverse so the truck slewed away fast.

Robbie looked down at Mags. The stubble didn't reach this far, so if he went she'd be okay. It was her or Fleet, but Fleet was nowhere to be seen, so he didn't need to make any decisions yet. He bent down to touch her neck.

No response. She was warm, at least.

This was how she'd said it would be, how she'd known it would be. So quick, so sharp, so neat.

People would be coming soon.

'Mags,' he hissed. 'Mags.'

There was a faint movement, a flicker of her eyelids. He stroked her hair, then rolled her over so the moonlight fell full on her face. Her eyes opened.

'Where am I?'

'How long have you got?'

'Is it over?'

Robbie looked up over her head.

'Not yet.'

Fleet was in the field again.

Mags followed his gaze.

When Fleet started to run he didn't think about staying. It was as if a voice in the back of his head was commanding him to go, go now. She didn't run too fast, because of the damage to her left leg. Even so, keeping up wasn't easy. Everywhere was light, it was like running along the underside of the surface of the sea in sunshine. Her whiteness blended like camouflage, but she was lolloping not belting, and she was going down the road between shining hedgerows, down past fields and crossroads. There was no one about, and soon they were among the outlying houses of the village. Robbie could see his house on the right, then the Allardyces', then he was down the road and passing the store, all the time wondering how long this was going to go on for, feeling like it could be forever. He didn't think he could do forever.

He saw her turning uphill, up the road to the church, and they were climbing again. He felt a surge of energy. He didn't know where it was coming from, but suddenly he thought maybe he could do forever after all.

The lights were on in the church, though it was empty. The door was wide open.

A movement caught his eye. In the graveyard among the moon-washed tombs were three solemn brown hares, sitting in a circle, their eyes on him. There was a feeling in the air, not kind, but not frightening either, like a stilled heartbeat, a suspension of things.

The universe was full of things he didn't understand. Dark energy. Dark matter. Dark matters.

And something was ending here, Robbie realized, in this churchyard, in this church, which was full of good old human light. Something that had happened many times before in the same place. A story that rolled like a wave or the curl of a whip though time and space, through seen and unseen, and there had never been anything anyone had ever been able to do to stop it.

He went into the church. The candles were lit. It felt warm and smelled of the benevolence of time.

Was he expecting to find Fleet sitting under the cross looking pleased with herself, or sorry for what she'd done?

She was nowhere to be seen. Maybe she hadn't come inside in the first place. Why would she? But he was sure he had seen her run in, and he was sure she was here somewhere.

He took his time walking up the aisle, squinting along the pews. In front of the altar he stopped. He thought about saying a prayer, but he'd never done that before, and he wasn't going to start now. Then he saw the vestry door was open, and the light was on. And he remembered Mags, radiant in the long mirror.

There was someone in the mirror this time too.

'Fran,' Robbie said.

She didn't say anything, she just looked at him. She was wearing a white dress, like the first time he'd seen her, and her left shin was covered in bright red blood. Robbie was shocked by the sight of it. It was a bad wound, but her face was peaceful and calm, not angry or sad or even happy. She wasn't locked in the past any more, and she didn't seem to be in any pain. And as he recovered himself, he remembered Mags's words when he'd seen Fran by the pool, about mirrors and dimensions and twinning. Fleet must be behind the door, he thought, but he knew he wasn't going to see her again in that shape. He could only see her reflection in the mirror, her original self, for a little while. And even as these thoughts came to him, Fran began to fade, but as she did so she was replaced by another woman, then another, just like outside the garage, and so many came so fast, a hurricane of faces, Robbie couldn't keep up with them, until one stayed.

His mum.

She looked peaceful too, and healthy. No illness wrinkles, no wrinkles at all. She was smiling at him.

And as they looked at each other, there was something new, a new feeling he experienced, and he didn't know what it meant, but it was as if she was telling him something. It was a feeling, and it was a thought.

It doesn't have to be this way, Robbie.

He didn't know whether she was saying this to him, or whether he was saying it to himself. But a deep peace spread through him, even as he raised his hand towards her, hoping to touch her, to stop her from going. Step out of the mirror and be with me again.

It doesn't have to be this way.

He knew what she meant, because he was remembering her letter, and he was no longer angry. As she faded away she smiled slightly and blew him a kiss, and in the church the lights began to dim. The candles were going out one by one, leaving the smell of wax heavy in the air. Slowly they were extinguished, and the lights were switching themselves off, and soon Robbie turned and he ran, through the darkening church that smelled of love into the warm bright night.

28

'BILLY STRICKLAND'S gone mad.'

They were down by the bridge.

'That doesn't surprise me.'

'He shakes his head and rolls his eyes and talks about hares and ghosts.'

'I know, Mags. Dad saw it on the local news. They didn't mention hares and ghosts, though. They just said he was insane.'

'What a way to go. Shot by your own brother.'

'You're lucky you didn't see it. It's me should be in the trauma ward.'

'Yeah. That was so weird. I felt so tired, it was like all my energy was being drawn out of me, and when I woke up I was left with all these crazy visions.'

'Visions? Visions of what?'

'Of fire, of running, of blood, of the moon, of a church. And the strangest one was seeing you.

I remember seeing you, staring at me. What was that about?'

For the first time with Mags, Robbie was the one with the answers.

'I think I was right. She needed you. She used you. For a little while, you were part of her. Your friend. She knew you wanted to help her and you did.'

'I'm not sorry. I'm not. I should be, but I'm not.'

Robbie hadn't told her everything about what had happened in the church. He would, eventually. But not just yet.

'Mags?' He was thinking about his mum's letter.

'Yes, Robbie?'

'What are the chime hours?'

'The chime hours. Okay. Chime hours. Or chiming hours. In the old days it was when the monks rang their bells. Why?'

'Nothing. Well, yeah, something. What was special about them?'

'The only thing I know is that if you are born during the chime hours, you have second sight. You can see things other people can't.'

'Is that when you were born?'

'I don't know. It's not why I'm the way I am.'

'Would Dad know about them?'

'It's well-known round here.'

'So he would.'

'When were you born, then?'

'It's something I need to talk about with Dad, but I can't.'

'It's bad the way you are with your dad. I said that to you. 'Specially as there's only him and you now.'

'It's better that way.'

'But it's still no good. Can't you forgive him?'

It was as if she could read his thoughts.

He could see his mum in the mirror, hear those words. *It doesn't have to be this way.*

He shook his head. 'No.' But it wasn't what he was feeling any more.

She sighed, and the water ran on under their feet.

'I'll bet you were born in the chime hours.'

'Yes,' he said. The letter, again. 'Yes. Maybe. What are people saying?'

'People in general, you mean? They can't take it in. Everyone thinks the boys were hunting, but no one can work out why they were burning stubble in the moonlight. Unless maybe to flush the animals out, but nobody does that any more. So in the end people think they were just being fruitloops. You know, they always were crazy. Another mad Strickland thing, only this time it went wrong. Poor Billy.'

'Poor Tommy.'

'Rough justice.'

'How's Mrs Strickland?'

'She's not been seen since. He was her prince. I feel sorry for her.'

'And what about the people who do know?'

'They're there. They'll always be there. Watching and waiting.'

'Your favourite phrase.'

'There's not much else you can do sometimes. There's lots of things happening you and me don't know about. 'Specially you.'

'Thanks.'

'Well, it's true. You might learn, though. And most of them you can't do much about, but some you can. That's something else you've got to learn. How to tell the difference.'

Robbie took the memory stick out of his pocket. It lay in the palm of his hand, innocent, ordinary.

'I thought I should do something about this. Still want it?'

'Yes.'

He flipped it over to her with his thumb. She reached for it, fumbled the catch, and had to jump down into the river after it.

'Ruined, I imagine,' she shouted up.

'Might be better that way,' he replied. 'You wouldn't like it much.'

She was splashing about in the river, her Converses soaked, the dark wet climbing up the legs of her jeans.

He looked down at her corn-coloured head.

'We didn't do much, did we?'

'You can't.' She started lobbing stones downriver,

lazily trying to hit a tree trunk that was leaning over the water. 'And –' she bent down to pick up more stones, brown and glistening from the river bed – 'it's not over.'

'Not over?'

'Believe me. Not over yet.' With every syllable she hurled a stone, then bent again for more from the cold rushing waters.

29

IN THE night Robbie swam out of a deep sleep. He knew something had woken him, but for several moments he didn't know where he was or even who he was. He reached to switch his bedside light on and nothing happened. There was light under the door, but for some reason it was flickering. Then he realized what it was that had woken him. It was the smell of burning.

And in his head he heard a voice. Mary Allardyce. Faint but getting louder and louder as the acrid smell filled his nostrils. *'It's said that when a hare runs through a village street a fire will break out in one of the houses very shortly afterwards.'*

It had taken its time, a couple of days or so. But here it was.

If he opened his door the air would feed the fire, but he had to, he had to take the chance.

The flames were climbing the walls of the stairwell. They had crossed the banisters that ran along the hall, and the blaze was building quickly between him and his dad's room. The clouds of smoke were so bad he had to shut his door immediately. There was no way through.

Dad.

'Dad!' he screamed.

There was no response.

He called again and again, but there was only the roaring of the fire.

He had to get out, and there was only one way.

Once he was through the window he hung on to the sill, swaying slightly from side to side, and then he took a breath and dropped, hit the ground and rolled. The moon was hidden by clouds, but there was enough light to see by. He called 999 on his phone and raced round the house until he was under his dad's window and he got through.

'Dad!'

'Can you just give me that address again, son?'

'Dad!'

'We'll have the fire service and an ambulance there in ten minutes. What was the name again?'

'Dad, can you hear me? Robbie, Robbie Lawton.'

'And the address? Can you just confirm that?' He did, hardly knowing what he was saying. All he knew was that there was no movement in his dad's room.

Smoke was billowing from the open window. He didn't have ten minutes.

Okay, Robbie, concentrate. There's a ladder in the shed.

The shed was locked, but he thought he could break in. He kicked hard against the door. It was tougher than he had thought and he was losing time. Another kick. It held.

With a yell of anger and hatred he took a run at it. To his astonishment the door splintered open. There was a stab of pain in his shoulder. He ignored it.

He couldn't see the ladder. He knew there was one in there, because he had seen his dad putting it away. He took a step back and fell over the lawn mower, to find himself staring up at the ladder, lying on struts that ran from one wall to another under the roof. He jumped up to grab the end rung, hoping his weight would tilt it so that it would slide down, but most of it was on the struts and was too heavy and that didn't work. He was panicking so much he could hardly see or think, then he saw a chair to stand on so he could pull the ladder properly, and it came cleanly.

He dragged it through the door, over the lawn and to the front. He put it against the wall of the house. After a while he could see the flames at the door of his dad's bedroom and the dark shape of a body in the bed.

He couldn't tell if he was still alive.

'Dad! Dad!'

Nothing.

He pushed himself through the window. He pulled the duvet off the bed and shouted in his dad's face.

'Dad! Come on, wake up!' His voice was rising to a shriek.

The smoke was suffocating, even with the windows wide open, and Robbie was beginning to choke.

He hooked his arms under his dad's shoulders and yanked, swinging him out of bed. How was he going to get him out of the window?

His dad's body was a dead weight, the smoke overpowering and the heat intense. Out of the corner of his eye he could see the door of the bedroom was beginning to go. He dragged his dad to the wall by the window, and climbed out. Then he leaned down and heaved. The pain in his shoulder felt like a bullet wound.

He had to push through the window into the smoke again. Leaning in, he lunged out and down to feel for his dad's body. Suddenly there was light beyond the smoke as the door went up in flames. Fire ballooned into the room. He ducked at the top of the ladder for a moment, recoiling from the heat, then forced himself back. At least he could see his dad better, slumped against the wall beneath him.

Okay, Robbie, lean in, push down and pull.

He was going to have to use his left arm, the right one was no good any more.

He couldn't do it. Too far, the pain too much.

Come on, Robbie, stretch. Stretch. You can do this.

He manoeuvred his hand under his dad's shoulder and round.

It's too hot, it's too hot.

His back felt like it was going to go. This just might be impossible.

Come on, Dad. I need you now. Come on, someone, somewhere.

Something shifted in his dad's weight. He was moving. He was alive. He was pushing himself back and up. He was coming with Robbie.

In one quick rush, as if they were bursting out of a flooded tank, his dad slid out of the window and they were falling, falling together, back down the ladder.

30

MAGS CAME to see him, and sat at the end of his hospital bed eating the grapes she'd brought.

'You were right, as usual,' he said. She raised her eyebrows at him. 'It wasn't over.'

She broke into that big grin. 'Well, you know what everyone's saying now.'

'What's that?'

She rolled her eyes, as if to say you're never going to believe this, but isn't it obvious?

'People think you started it. 'Cos of your conviction.'

'You're kidding me. I started a fire in my own home?'

'That's what they're saying. You've got form, remember?'

'My conviction? Do you know what my conviction is, Mags? My conviction is your village is mad. And I am being kind.'

'Well, it's only a few people. Anyway, what did happen? There are lots of other rumours. Mice at the wiring, that kind of thing.'

'Some electrical fault, that's what I've been told. Can mice do that?'

'I don't know. Anyway, you didn't.'

There was something in her tone Robbie couldn't quite get, some implication.

'Are you thinking someone else did?'

'Not someone.'

'You think the fire happened because she ran through the village?'

'Well, she did.'

'You don't think it was a freak accident?'

'I don't. You know it wasn't.'

'If you say so.'

'I do say so. Anyway, when's your dad out?'

'I don't know.' He thought about when he first saw him after the fire. It had been a bad fall. 'It'll be a while.'

'Do you want to come and stay at ours if you're out first?'

Robbie couldn't think of anything worse than staying at Mags's with her crazy mother.

'Yeah,' he said. 'That'd be cool.'

When his dad emerged from hospital and came to pick him up and take him to their temporary home

Robbie could have kissed him. In fact, he did. His dad looked surprised, then gave him the most enormous hug. He didn't kiss him back, but he'd learn, thought Robbie. Things were going to be different, they really were.

His dad's insurance meant they had a new place to stay in while the old house was repaired. It wasn't too far away, but it was good to have a break from the village for a while. And as they slowly regained their strength in the new place, just the two of them, they both began to lose that sense of their past pressing down upon them. They were cautious with each other – but they both knew some threshold had been crossed, some new world entered, and though neither knew what was in it, they were glad to be there.

Then one day as his dad served up fish fingers and peas for dinner Robbie noticed he seemed unusually quiet and thoughtful.

'Robbie,' he said, taking a deep breath, as if he was trying to cure hiccups. 'I've been meaning to ask you something. That letter from your mum.'

'Yes?'

'What did it say?'

'Do you want to read it?'

His dad looked eager and nervous at the same time.

'Could I? I mean, would you?'

Robbie thought back. 'I was right, wasn't I, about why you hid it?'

His dad pulled a face. 'Well, like I said, I was worried about what it might do to you, because I didn't know what she'd written. I didn't think I should open it myself. And, yes, of course you were right, of course I was scared. Petrified, if you want to know.'

His son shook his head slowly. 'I'm not sure I want to show it to you, Dad. I don't see why I should. You hid it from me.'

His dad nodded. 'I know. And then we had a fight and I shouldn't have talked to you like that. I'm sorry.'

'Why did you put it in that book between the pages about the white hare?'

His dad's head jerked up and he stared at Robbie in consternation. 'Did I? How strange.' His eyes narrowed, and his fingers traced patterns across his forehead as he tried to remember. Then he looked tentatively at Robbie. 'There's a legend about the white hare round here. You probably don't know it. Maybe you do. Mags might have told you. She tells you everything, doesn't she?'

'Not everything. Just what she needs to.'

He looked at his son again, cradling his chin in his hand. 'Did she tell you about that one?'

'When a woman dies abandoned by her lover,' Robbie intoned. 'Yes.' He let the silence reign between them. Then, 'Dad?'

'Yes?'

'It wasn't about you.'

His dad rolled his eyes and laughed, a little too loudly.

'No, of course not. Well, let's forget the letter. I shouldn't have asked.' He got up to clear the plates, trying unsuccessfully to whistle.

Robbie leaned back on his chair, put his hands behind his head, took a deep breath, righted himself, then went upstairs and returned with the letter in his hand.

'Dad?'

'Yes?' His dad came out of the kitchen and saw what Robbie was holding.

'You know you said you were frightened of what she might have written?'

His dad's expression turned to wariness. 'Yes?'

'You needn't have been.'

He laid it flat on the table, smoothing out the creases, and they read it together.

DARLING ROBBIE,

If you are reading this, don't be too sad. I have asked your dad to give this letter to you when I'm no longer here, and I'm afraid it seems as if that time is not so far away. You have always been the world to me, Robbie, and it breaks my heart not to see you grow up. I can't help thinking about your future, and how I won't be there for it. I won't be there to help you when your own heart gets broken, or to make sure you do the right thing when you break someone else's; I won't be there when you get married, if you do, or help you with your children, if you have them. I won't be there to show you the upside of down when things go wrong, however small, like if I buy you the wrong colour shirt on an impulse, or give you a friendship bracelet that embarrasses you, or large, like if you get divorced, or wreck a car, or worse. You could fail your exams, you could get fired from your job, you could do brilliantly (which of course I know you will). When you get angry (which you do, too much, I think, you'll need to watch that) I won't be there to calm you, when you lose faith in yourself I won't be able to help you find it again. I won't be able to help you find what books to read or films to see whatever age you are, and believe me I'd go on doing it, or what biscuits to eat when you feel like an indulgence or what herbs to put on roast lamb (rosemary, and lots of it; don't bother with anything else). I won't be there to tell you when you've done well, or hint, best as I can, that you could have done better.

Think of me, though, loving you constantly from afar, from wherever I am going. You're a beautiful boy, Robbie, and I can't make up my mind which bit of you I love most – that curling hair which you won't let me stroke so I have to wait until you're asleep, those long lashes, that lightning turn of speed, your soft skin, the way you blush when you get cross, your dark eyes which somehow have colours swimming in them, the way you sing to yourself around the house and we sometimes sang together, the scar on your knee that you got when you were small, the way your eyebrows meet when you're concentrating, or the way your nose scrunches up when you don't like something. You've got lots of attitude, Robbie, and I love that most of all, I think, but like your anger you're going to have to learn to deal with it. See them both for what they are: wild horses you'll have to tame to survive. That is my greatest wish for you, apart from the obvious, which is that you will be loved and admired and cherished by the world the way I know you should be.

And look after your dad. He's a good man, most of the time, but he can be a bit hopeless. I know all about Sheila. I'm not against her, knowing what I know. I like her; she's been a friend to me too. She has my blessing, and I have encouraged the two of them, which might surprise you (and your dad). Sharing the making of a child, who will have a whole life all the way from the beginning to the inevitable end, is an amazing thing, and that never goes away, and perhaps that's part of it. Your dad is terrified of the future, of losing me, of being alone. But it is more important to me, Robbie, that you take care of each other. You will both need each other, and it won't do any good to be bitter towards him, as I think you might be. Men need women (and sometimes vice versa), it's as simple as that, and if it's not me, or Sheila, it will be someone else. But fathers also need their sons, and sons do need their fathers.

Grow well and work hard and go on being the son to be proud of that I have always loved so very completely, my darling, darling boy.

All my love,
Mum

P.S. Ask your dad about the chime hours. You were always special.

It was hard to read however many times Robbie had read it since that evening in the church. His dad was not saying anything. Robbie put his arm gently across his shoulders.

'She was wrong, though,' said Robbie. 'I wouldn't have understood what she was saying. It's better now than then. She wouldn't have approved of the arson either, would she? Criminal conviction for her beloved son?'

'I asked Mags about the chime hours,' Robbie said later, when his dad had calmed down and Robbie had recovered from the shock of seeing him in tears. 'It's about when you're born, isn't it?'

'Oh, yes, well, you were born between midnight and dawn on a Saturday morning, two o'clock I think it was, and I remembered this old superstition they have round here. Another one! If you're born during the chime hours, when the monks used to ring their bells, you're apparently supposed to have, what is it called, second sight. You can see things others can't, parallel worlds, ghosts, all that sort of thing. A bit like the white hare.' He stopped and frowned, and looked at Robbie thoughtfully. Then he smiled to himself. 'We used to laugh about that. I don't know why I remembered it. I think it was probably that old grandfather clock of ours chiming away in the dead of night.'

'I sometimes think you remember more than you let on, Dad.'

'Do you? I don't think I do. What do I remember?' He paused. 'I remember you and I going to see films, Robbie. It's a terribly long time since we did that. We should do it again.'

'And fishing.'

'Yes, oh, yes. Now, you know, Robbie, that's a bit of an idea. I've still got my kit somewhere, it was in the shed, so the fire didn't get to it. I might just go and dig it out again. It'll need an overhaul, but then everything does every now and then. I don't suppose you'd want to come with me nowadays, though?'

'Well, you never know. I might. Now and then. If you let me off gardening.'

His dad nodded happily. 'Good. Anyway. The chime hours. Well, that's one thing you didn't really need to know from that letter, isn't it?' He opened his eyes wide. 'Some letter, all right.'

And he smiled again, this time at Robbie.

Author Note and Acknowledgements

I owe a great deal to *The Leaping Hare* by George Ewart Evans and David Thomson. I bought it in the school bookshop when I was fourteen, but didn't read it until I began thinking about writing a book of this nature some decades later. It has been a rich resource, for which I am very grateful.

I am also grateful to Anthony Cheetham for his alacrity and enthusiasm, my astonishing editor Fiona Kennedy, my wonderful readers Katrin Williams and Barnaby Fishwick, my brilliant cover designer Emma Ewbank, my copy-editor Jenny Glencross, Caradoc King, Sam Taylor, Samuel Fishwick, David Miller, Megan Schaffer, Catherine Clarke, Christelle Chamouton, Jon Dunn, Sarah Whitehouse, Jonathan Taylor and the lovely and supportive people at Head of Zeus, including the insightful Madeleine O'Shea, Jessie Price, Suzanne Sangster, Clémence Jacquinet, Ian Rutland and Amanda Ridout.

Michael Fishwick
London
January 2017